The Diva and Me

The Diva and Me

Mahir Salih

CONTENTS

Chapter 1	Across the English Channel 2015	1
Chapter 2	Paris, *je t'aime*	5
Chapter 3	Campe de la lande	10
Chapter 4	Poor Paris	17
Chapter 5	Another Paris	21
Chapter 6	East meets West	25
Chapter 7	Clash of Stags	29
Chapter 8	Getting out of Hell	36
Chapter 9	Tomorrow is Another World	40
Chapter 10	Hopes and Aspirations	43
Chapter 11	Clash of the Mountains	47
Chapter 12	Leaving Paradise	52
Chapter 13	The Fall from Grace	55
Chapter 14	Lost Everything	58
Chapter 15	Hard Times	61
Chapter 16	The Eminent Union	65
Chapter 17	Back to the Stage	69
Chapter 18	The Web of Deceit	72
Chapter 19	The Summit	78
Chapter 20	Glamour to Belleville	81
Chapter 21	Life like Others	86
Chapter 22	Come and Dine with Me	90
Chapter 23	Another Day, a Different Day	95
Chapter 24	Let's Sing	98
Chapter 25	Life is Full of Surprises	103
Chapter 26	In Preparation for the Great Night	108

Chapter 27	Life is a Roller Coaster	112
Chapter 28	No Pride in Time of Need	115
Chapter 29	The Night of her Life	118
Chapter 30	Nuit de César	120
Chapter 31	Convalescence after the Scandal	126
Chapter 32	On the Way to the Côte d'Azur	129
Chapter 33	Break at the Côte d'Azur	132
Chapter 34	It is a Holiday	136
Chapter 35	Night out in Saint Tropez	143
Chapter 36	Back to Paris	148
Chapter 37	The Fruits of Success	152
Chapter 38	A Painful Journey	155
Chapter 39	La vie en Rose	159
Chapter 40	New Start	165
Chapter 41	Action Time	168
Chapter 42	The Escape Plan	171
Chapter 43	Meeting in Bois De Boulogne	174
Chapter 44	Planning is Ongoing	177
Chapter 45	Gare Du Nord (All Aboard)	179

Chapter One

Across the English Channel 2015

On a bright day with clear skies at the end of summer and early autumn, the sea was blue and the skies were clear, which was unusual at that time of the year. It was an exception after the unpredictable weather in recent years which had been attributed to global warming.

An inflatable boat, designed for leisure and tranquil river cruises, but not for the busiest water strait in the world was crossing the channel peacefully. The boat was heavy with five men and a woman. A weight well beyond its acceptable capacity for passengers. The human cargo comprised people from different nationalities. Three olive-skinned men were talking in low voices in an incomprehensible language that resembled Arabic. They had fled the horrendous war atrocities in Syria and wished to reach the peaceful English shores.

A couple hanging on to each other were wearing fake Nike tracksuits and had protected themselves with heavy water-resistant coats. They had flown all the way from China, after fleeing oppression and they were in search of a better life in the West. Also fleeing to the UK were a newlywed couple. The girl's abdomen indicated the early months of pregnancy.

Karim was young man in his mid-thirties. As he spoke angrily his pearly-white teeth were in contrast to his olive skin, dark hair and dishevelled beard. He was a Syrian refugee who'd had enough of the poor conditions — a rogue smuggler of human cargo had received shipping money in advance from poor refugees who were his victims.

Nevertheless, Karim had been rescued from appalling living conditions and enforced humiliation at the jungle camp near Calais where he had been for almost two years, living in a tent made of leftover plastic and cardboard cartons with no bathing or toilet facilities.

The boat's occupants carried their dreams for start a fresh, a new life in the UK, where they hoped to find jobs and start a family or trace their long-lost families. The boat dwellers had one thing in common — the desire to be treated as humans. They came from different parts of the world — Syria, Afghanistan, Pakistan, China, and were fleeing war, persecution and poverty, seeking a better life in the West.

Two strong young men were rowing to the English shores, and as they avoided British navy patrols, they were not much concerned about the French authorities because they seemed happy to close their eyes and allow them to pass with subtle blessings.

While the boat's occupants were dreaming for their new life, thunder in the sky woke them from their daydreams and jolted them to bitter reality. A storm hit the calm sea and waves rose from gentle to giant and aggressive. The boat could not cope with the turbulent sea. The noise of the storm revived Karim's plight and suffering and he relived the war around Aleppo, where he refused to join either side — the Assad regime or the opposition with the ongoing name changes from Nusrat Allah to Islamic State, to Daesh, to Islamic Estate of the Fertile Crescent. Different names but the same people and the same outcome — destruction.

Karim wanted to raise his two children in peace and educate them to the best of his ability so they could have a normal decent life, but this was impossible to achieve in a war zone.

The sea was suspiciously calm and quiet. Too good to be true. The rowers rowed with immense force to reach their dream land. A few hours after ceasing their activity to avoid the commercial carriers and the coastguard patrols, the wind velocity increased. The fragile (not fit for the purpose), boat lost its balance in the face of the oncoming waves of the increasingly disturbed sea.

The rowers stopped rowing immediately. The noise of the waves hitting the boat mingled with shouts of the passengers, who were asking for mercy from a higher power.

Karim blocked his ears to the cries of the others as he felt the bitter coldness of chilled salty seawater that filled the boat and entered his sinuses.

Not long after, the boat capsized and the swimmers were the winners.

Terror was etched on the faces of passengers. The pregnant Middle Eastern woman clung in fear to her husband as she tried to protect her unborn baby from drowning. Her partner tried to keep her afloat with no success. She was snatched away by a vicious cold wave. The others were indifferent to her shouts and pleas for help. While her husband was intent on saving himself. The two Arabs held each other firmly until they realised that their union would mean their end. They pushed each other away as they shouted like a child seeking the security of his mother. The Asian couple were separated on either side of the boat. And the Chinese girl was left alone shouting words in her native tongue as she hoped in vain to be rescued.

Karim tried to swim ashore, and as he did he imagined a film trailer with Paris the city he admired because of its charm from the daytime glamour of the buildings and the monuments to the spectacular lights during the night. It lived up to its reputation as *the City of Lights* (La Cité de la Lumière). Parisians and tourists alike enjoyed leisurely days with spectacular scenery, amazing architecture, museums and churches instead of the horrors of war in his native country Syria.

He woke to the desperate cries for help from a girl shouting in a language he did not comprehend. All he understood was that she was seeking help. There is no language barrier when death comes that close. He had prided himself as the best swimmer in the Euphrates River, but he could not grasp the young girl who was screaming. Her will to live was stronger than her swimming skills. Eventually she hung on to Karim and dragged him down deep, but his survival instinct made him push her away, but then he tried to grab her to control her fierce jerky struggles that seemed disproportionate to her tiny feeble body. His survival instinct was strong. Flashbacks of his wife and children attacked him. He kept repeating, 'I will live. I will live.' The water was freezing. Karim's limbs had gone numb and he had lost a degree of sensation. He was shivering uncontrollably when in the distance, he saw a light and heard a whistle. The light and the sound faded away. He thought about his deceased mother and called her name in a low-pitched voice. He was ready to meet her. Just then, he recognised a few words in French that were coming from men in uniforms before he fell into a deep sleep.

Chapter two

Paris, *je t'aime*

Autumn came early to Paris. The leaves had fallen from the trees that lined both sides of the street and covered the pavement of the Champs-Élysées. But the glamour of this beautiful city never ceased all year around. The city swam at night, the lights, restaurants and night life. There was something for everyone. The serenity of the eternal Seine River gave the noisy city a tranquil break.

At the exclusive Châtelet neighbourhood in the centre of Paris and opposite to the square of Saint-Jacques tower, a state of the art eighteenth-century building stood upright against all odds.

Inside the building, on the second floor, was a huge flat consisting of four bedrooms, two drawing rooms and three bathrooms. The apartment was spacious for one person. The entire walls of the living room were ornamented with photos of a young, beautiful, sexy woman. The depiction of a previous glorious life. The Louis Fourteen XIV furniture spoke of an era and an owner who was in continuous denial of her true age.

Having of husbands and boyfriends. Her memories recounted an exciting life that she never wanted to end.

With time, her beauty and fame, and even money had been exhausted and her family and friends had disappeared. She had been lucky to keep her exclusive flat and some investments provided her with a modest income.

She was Sandrine, the French cinema diva of the 1960s and 1970s. She once had beauty and acting talent that won her César's awards and she had also been nominated for an Oscar as best foreign actress. Her contribution extended to English-speaking films that she mastered in the hope of joining the elite of Hollywood. Alas, she made only a few films in Hollywood before she was made redundant but she was the *darling* of the Francophone world. Nevertheless, she had been a star competing with big names such as Catherine Deneuve and even Brigitte Bardot.

Time had gone by and her good looks had faded. Her talent granted her only a few roles in French films to play the part of an older mother, but her pride prevented her from accepting anything but the role of the young protagonist. When the diva declined many roles eventually the producers and fans forgot her. Her devotion to her career was everything, and she refused to start a family or even maintain a relationship with her endless star prosperous but not exclusive life. Her diva characteristics and some narcissistic traits shut her off from the world. She spent her days in the park walking her Staffordshire dog Lulu, ruminating on old long-gone memories or watching TV paying more attention to her old films with a glass of white wine in her hand. Her only companion apart from her dog Lulu was her glass of alcoholic beverage.

Occasionally, she responded to the landline phone when it rang; usually it was the odd old friend or maybe a fan. She had maintained her slim figure by depriving herself of high carbohydrate foods and replaced them with white wine and caviar. The latter was replaced with cottage cheese when she got into financial difficulties and had to self-impose austere living. Her drinking level had reached the degree where she could not carry on her day without it. There was nothing more terrifying to her than standing on the scales or even worse, looking in the mirror. She had lost count of the wrinkles covering her face; each represented an eventful year of her life. Her look was all that mattered but not the wisdom that came with it. *"Brain and beauty are forever in conflict,"* was a comment she recalled during a discussion with the prominent feminist writer Françoise Sagan in the 1960s.

Despite the fact that French cinema is generally treated as an art and older experienced actresses continue to give the audience a marvellous performance, the studios found it difficult to work with her.

Sandrine longed for the days of her youth when she ruled the studios like the Billancourt in Paris in their heydays.

She lay back on the engraved wooden Indian lounger and rang the porcelain bell next to her.

A middle-aged woman who walked with a hunchback, and struggled to walk and talk had been summoned by the bell. She was a Bulgarian who came to France looking for a better life but could not find a job to match her high qualifications. Anna could not leave her pride at home after a history of twenty years as a primary school teacher.

Sandrine spoke with her proud, strong Parisian accent in an assertive tone as she gave orders to her maid who swallowed this insult because she received a salary that was double the one she had received at home as a teacher.

'Mon boisson,' said Sandrine meaning the Champagne she drank early in the morning instead of eating breakfast, particularly the baguette and croissant that she loved and hated.

The poor women shuffled towards the kitchen, murmuring swear words in Bulgarian that were directed towards Sandrine. She acknowledged Sandrine's hatred of foreigners. Sandrine often voiced her opinion about the invasion of France by foreigners. She had shamelessly published open letters to the media and French dignitaries about the alien invasion by others, especially Muslims, and her fear of them influencing the French way of life.

Sandrine picked up her smartphone and tried to access her What's App account without success. She wanted to get a message to her agent François who had given her endless instructions on how to operate the bloody phone. *'Merde,'* she uttered the swear word in disgust and picked up the landline next to her and dialled a number she knew by heart.

'Allo, is that you François?'

'Yes chérie. Bonjour. How are you?'

'What do you expect? I am a woman who has lost everything as you see.'

'You have good health; that's what matters.'

'*Oui,* not love though. *Alors,* my loneliness is not what I am calling about. Have you spoken to Duval?'

'Who is Duval?'

'What is wrong with you? Duval, the producer.'

'Of course, sorry. I forgot to tell you that he is offering you some work.'

Sandrine's heart began pounding like a steam train engine. She had been waiting for an acting opportunity for long time. She swallowed her pride. 'Who is acting with me?' she asked in a diva tone. Her attitude had been the same when she used to have the chance to choose and sack actors, who might or might not play roles with her. She was the diva after all.

Francois realised the trap he had fallen into. 'It is a role that is very important to the plot.'

'What is that?'

'You will be the mother of the female protagonist.' His voice was diminished as if had been struck by lightning.

There was a long pause. *How dare he? I am the only protagonist and always will be.*

'Why the mother?' She spat in a harsh rude voice.

'Well, that is what they have.'

She did not want it. 'The problem is not with what they have but with you fool.'

'Madame, roles come and go and it is not the same as thirty or forty years ago.' His words came out as if he had a frog in his throat.

'I will find another agent. You are useless,' she yelled.

'Sandrine listen …' he said in an irritated voice.

She was plagued with extreme nervousness knowing she was avoiding a major point — admitting the reality of her age and her long-gone youth. She stared at the mirror. *'Mon Dieu,'* she shouted. What had happened to the gorgeous girl who all the world's kings and presidents wished a minute or so with. She remembered vividly how the French Government begged her to speak nicely to an African president to save her country billions of francs and the Arab sheik who offered to marry her temporarily and give her unlimited funds to cover her expenses as well as those who would inherit from her.

Now, the facelift and the recurrent Botox was not working.

She declined roles as a mother, her excuse being that she'd never had children. Just then she had an intrusive flashback of going to the private Parisian clinic forty years ago and asking the obstetrician to terminate her pregnancy. 'Doctor, it must be done now. I have a contract to start shooting in South America soon,' she'd said. He'd tried to convince her of the risk that she might not be able to bear any more children.

Sandrine woke from her day's nightmare and burst into tears and asked forgiveness for the lost child. She was a non-practising Catholic, but her deep-rooted guilt stemmed from her mother and grandmother's strong religious beliefs. Her youthful beauty had long gone and she was alone.

Her dog Lulu came closer to her and licked her face as if he was telling her she was not alone and she was loved unconditionally. 'My baby.' She held him tight. *Alone with no love*. She mumbled as she looked at her face on the mirror.

Chapter three

Campe de la lande

In an early morning of 2016, a group of men emerged from between tents or huts made from cartons and redundant, recycled plastic material. The place was close to the French port of Calais in northern France.

Families from war-battered or poverty-stricken countries such as Syria, Iraq, Afghanistan, Africa, Pakistan etc were gathered in ghettos categorised by their countries, affiliations or needs. Families lived under the same roof if the weather permitted, and if the carton and plastic huts survived the ghastly wind and torrential rain. There were no essential facilities such as toilets, baths or kitchens, and people slept head to foot on the floor in close proximity without any privacy. The refugees were discussing with loud voices their dismay at their treatment by French authorities and their difficulties in learning French, plus the disappointment of integrating with French society.

Rogue smugglers were spread everywhere like vultures preying on the poor and the vulnerable people who were desperate to reach their dream destination for a better life in the United Kingdom. Some had heard positive feedback about

Copyright © 2022 by Mahir Salih.

ISBN:	Softcover	978-1-6641-1780-8
	eBook	978-1-6641-1781-5

All rights reserved. No part of this book may be reproduced or transmitted in any form or by any means, electronic or mechanical, including photocopying, recording, or by any information storage and retrieval system, without permission in writing from the copyright owner.

This is a work of fiction. Names, characters, places and incidents either are the product of the author's imagination or are used fictitiously, and any resemblance to any actual persons, living or dead, events, or locales is entirely coincidental.

Any people depicted in stock imagery provided by Getty Images are models, and such images are being used for illustrative purposes only.
Certain stock imagery © Getty Images.

Print information available on the last page.

Rev. date: 05/31/2022

To order additional copies of this book, contact:
Xlibris
UK TFN: 0800 0148620 (Toll Free inside the UK)
UK Local: (02) 0369 56328 (+44 20 3695 6328 from outside the UK)
www.Xlibrispublishing.co.uk
Orders@Xlibrispublishing.co.uk

living and integrating with British society. This was the main bonus that they expected after fleeing persecution and they hoped to give themselves and their children a better life. Many of the refugees had paid their life savings or sold their own or family's property and jewellery and had to work like slaves to pay their debts. The debt was paid by hard labour, with others engaged in prostitution or any other exploitative job to cover their endless debts compounded by extortionate interest which was impossible to pay.

The Red Cross station was small and had been a non-existent presence until the world's uproar and cries reached the international society and media about the derelict living conditions of the refugees in the jungle camp which was not fit for human habitation. The international media was renowned for exploiting the disgusting way this disadvantaged population from countries blighted by wars, catastrophes, natural disasters, and political oppression were suffering. International celebrity attention helped tremendously to bring world media attention to the Calais jungle.

Faces with different looks and different colours met you with smile, but despite the smiling faces they were stricken with great trepidation of the unknown. Every now and then a few faces disappeared from the camp, followed by rumours of their arrival in the land of milk and honey or their deaths in the deep-blue sea. Stories of capsized boats were common, and not heard so often by French or British media. Some of the fugitives were detained by authorities across the English Channel, if they were lucky.

Karim underwent a through, agonising interrogation by French authorities after his miraculous escape from an imminent death. He was questioned about his motivation to embark on such a dangerous journey which would more than likely end up in the unknown.

French interrogators kept repeating the same questions, showing no interest in knowing the facts, but more willing to show who was the boss. They did not succeed. The major item of interest was the disappearance of the Asian girl who went missing when the boat capsized before they were rescued by the French coastguard. He recalled a disturbing flashback that he had to live with.

'I swam towards her. She was struggling,' Karim said to the interrogator who seemed to be indifferent to the whole subject, having been desensitised by with endless cases he had come across.

'You could be a suspect if she is dead.' The French interrogator muttered the words with no interest in the impact on the poor terrified man.

'I had nothing to do with that. You should be looking for the real culprit — the smuggler,' Karim hissed as he tried to clear his throat.

The interrogator was a young French man from Normandy whose neighbourhood was fed up with refugee stories that were a common subject at dinner tables. The interrogator terminated the interview by announcing his need to get a French-Arabic interpreter because he was not interested in conducting the interview in English. Karim had tried to learn English at school, but it was not good enough to communicate, so he tried to listen to YouTube and read whatever available English books he could as he planned to build a new life abroad.

That evening Karim returned to the carton hut he was sharing with other four inmates. He was not surprised to learn three of them had disappeared. He wished that the French authorities had locked him in prison with better living conditions or at least that he had a bed of his own. He tried to sleep, but he was tormented by the vivid images of the gasping girl who had been hanging on to him, drawing him into the sea. She haunted him in nightmares.

He had dreamt of going to London from a young age. In his imagination, London was the trendy city inhabited by trendy people as per depictions in films. Despite being gobsmacked by the beauty of the architecture and the elegance of Parisians, London was the alleged land of tolerance according to information from other immigrants who were successful in reaching British shores. His short stay in Paris had not been encouraging when he encountered right-wing people, but equally, he had been looked after by French people there who had been very sympathetic. His thoughts diverted back to the jungle camp which had been reducing gradually in number because it was being dispersed by the French authorities. The majority of the refugees were single men. The camp contained less families than before. The unfortunate incidents that were occurring were a deterrent to families. Some had settled elsewhere in France, while very few had managed to successfully cross La Manche, as the French called the English Channel.

In the morning, after an unrestful night Karim was looking for his old time mates who he had bonded with, when he caught a glimpse of his fellow countryman and friend Jamal.

'Jamal is that you?'

Jamal turned as he tried to fix his glasses, to adjust his vison. His prescription was overdue for an update.

'Karim, is that you? *Alhamdulillah*! You are alive. I was worried sick about you.'

'Thank God, I am alive. God saved me from certain doom,' Karim added.

'I heard that everyone in that boat has gone.'

'I know one or two have survived. The rests' fate is unknown.' Karim burst into tears and Jamal hugged him dearly.

'You are alive. I have not spoken to your wife as I promised you because I was not sure if I should.'

'Thank you. My wife, Fadwa, would have died if she learnt of my ordeal. I have not spoken to her for over a week.'

Jamal watched over his shoulder, before he produced a small mobile phone. So far he had managed to hide it from other fellow refugees who would ask him to call their families. Jamal beckoned for Karim to follow him outside the carton and plastic huts where no eyes were watching. Karim had become the camp's star after surviving his recent adventure and was often surrounded by the young men asking him about his trip, inquiring about the dos and don'ts. They were not deterred by the consequences regardless of the misadventure he had endured.

Karim knew his wife's mobile number by heart, and Jalal tried to divert the young men's attention by talking about a runaway plan, but he decided to leave him in peace while he was trying to dial relentlessly until after a few attempts he finally succeeded.

A soft feminine voice came from other side spoke, '*Salaam alaykum.*'

'*Marhaba.*'

'Karim, is that you? Thank God. How are you? Where are you? I've worried stiff about you. Each time I watch the news someone ...' He heard her voice fading away and mixed with grunts.

'Please Fadwa, keep calm. I am fine love.'

'Come back, Karim. We need you. The kids miss you. We spend a great deal of the day in the shelters,' she said.

He realised that Fadwa was pushed to the limit and there was the possibility that the call was being censored. Karim changed the subject. 'How are Ahmed and Randa?'

'The children are fine. Looking forward to seeing you. Ahmed should have started intermediate school next month but going to school is uncertain. Randa is struggling. She has started wetting her bed.'

Karim wanted to pass on that subject and ask about his dearest daughter who he was very close to. 'What about Randa? Is she okay?'

'She asks about you all the time. I want to take her out of this hell.'

Before he was able to reply the line was cut off. He was not sure if it was just the weak network performance or the government censorship. He was deeply concerned about his family's fate, but he comforted himself with the fact that Turkish authorities were kinder than the Syrian ones.

He felt the need to pack and go back home, leaving the life of misery in the jungle and the promised paradise in the UK.

A trailer of his past life played in his mind after having to leave his birth country at the end of the Arab uprising that enflamed so much of the Middle East and took another turn in his native Syria. A brutal civil war had erupted and there was no end to it once the Western powers made a power vacuum by invading Iraq. This caused the expansion of Iranian influence where everybody was fighting each other.

Pre-war, his life had been stable. He had qualified as a maths' teacher, got married to the woman he loved, and had two lovely children and he had looked after his parents until their death. He was the ideal son that everyone wished to have.

He'd had to leave in haste, after being reported to have thoughts and potential activities against the regime during the civil war. There was no time for him to decide to stay or take his wife and the children along with him.

"Where will you go? Its uncharted territories," his wife had said. "We will suffer without you," she had added.

"But more so with me," he had replied.

The trailer continued starting with his journey to Turkey where he was interrogated by the authorities. He'd had to live off scarce resources and begged at times until he was registered with the United Nations as a refugee. He followed the exodus of Syrians and other refugees to Greece transported by DIY boats made of plastic. Many times they were followed by the Greek coastguard and sent back to Turkey but finally, he succeeded in getting there. He had endured the worst possible living conditions. Days and nights sleeping outdoors and putting up with extreme weather conditions. He walked on foot across Europe, at times using public transport and at other times he had to sneak across borders between countries.

He became stuck in Hungary while he was imprisoned in Budapest for no reason except that he was fleeing war and persecution. However, his plan had to continue. He opted to head to France despite the protest of his mates whose plan was to go to Germany, and benefit from the relaxed asylum laws and the generosity of the German benefit system.

'France is not the place to settle in,' a travel companion hissed in his ear.

'It is not France I wanna head to but England.'

As he came back from his daydream, he realised that fact. He was stuck in France.

Chapter four

Poor Paris

On an early autumn day, Paris could never have been prettier. The brown leaves falling from the horse chestnut trees were spread along the streets near the Tuileries Palace. In central Paris the park was a joy and one of the most popular tourist attractions. Much to their horror, the breeze was messing up many Parisian women's hairstyles. Slender women with stiletto-heeled shoes made by French designers were moving in haste to catch the Metro to work. It was part of being Parisian. Those with a lower income bought a cheaper version of these fashion shoes. Men were wearing suits without matching ties as the old French fashion style from the past dictated. People hurried to catch the Metro or buses without taking notice of each other. The Metro was full with passengers, most likely on their way to La Défense where the Paris business district is situated.

Meanwhile, tourists and the culture worshippers were flocking from all over the continents towards the centre of Paris, pleasuring their senses with the Arc du Triomphe, Place de la Concorde, Place Vendôme and the Champs-Élysées. The richer shoppers aimed towards Galeries Lafayette to indulge in buying the latest famous designers products. The less fortunate ones opted for stands in Belleville. In the centre of Belleville was a food stall managed by Haji an Algerian immigrant in his late fifties, who wore a traditional Algerian jilbab, and shouted to draw the client's attention to taste his food products. His parents worked with the French authorities in pre-independent Algeria thus they were classified as traitors by the post-independence Algerian Government and were the same as the Pieds-noirs who were forced to flee post-independent Algeria in 1962. His stall was full of Middle-Eastern food which was increasingly popular in France rather than North African food. He stocked hummus, baba ghanoush and falafels, which had been recently discovered by the French palate. It was heaven to those who had become vegans. Karim approached the stall with a smile.

Salaam alaykum,' Karim's smile was so infectious that Haji replied with a broader one. *'Alaykum salaam.* Would you like to try my products?'

Karim looked with hungry eyes despite his doubts that an Algerian could produce them as tasty as the Syrian made ones. Haji showed full sympathy when he heard Karim's story of trying to flee to England without success. He had chosen Paris as a last resort because there were few of his fellow countrymen and there was more cash in hand from work opportunities.

He counted his euros, his weekly allowance from the social security since he had been granted the permission to stay in France. He had enough to buy a bus ticket and a simple meal of bread and vegetables. He had been sharing a hotel room with other refugees in a derelict rundown hotel in Belleville where there were no cooking facilities. Haji offered him food in a generous spirit. 'It is on me. Please help yourself, dig in.'

But Karim's pride could not accept the offer. 'Thank you, I am not hungry. I have just eaten.'

Haji had come across many immigrants and refugees from North Africans to Egyptians to Iraqis, and now Syrians. He understood their plight and their pride. A few had made it in the UK but the majority had not. Haji ushered Karim to come closer and whispered in his ear. 'Do you want to work?' His words came as if he was revealing classified information.

Karim pride was hit hard, being unemployed was out of character for a decent man according to tradition. 'Yes, I would love to. I was a teacher in my country,' he replied immediately.

Haji glanced at him and touched his shoulder lightly. 'Listen, you are like my young brother. I have spent the majority of my life in this country. Look around you, do you see a white face here?'

'No,' Karim replied after a rapid scan of the place.

'This is the maximum you can get as a job in France. My family are literally French. All they can get are cleaning jobs and if they are lucky a trade job like me.'

Karim could not swallow his pride anymore. 'No way. I am a respectable man. I am teacher. I swear to God,' he blurted out as tears jumped from his hazel eyes.

'I believe you, friend. I have seen medical doctors and ministers in your place. It is not dishonourable to work, and if you want to earn more respect and money to help your family back home who suffer the worst horror of war, which is poverty.'

Karim moved from the thinker's position emulating Rodin's sculpture to a realistic and practical pose. 'Okay, what kind of job?'

'It is management of a house or you can call yourself a helper.'

'A servant, you mean?' he asked with a start of surprise.

'We are all servants of God. No, it is manager of a house that belongs to rich French people. They are looking for someone who is good at repairs, someone to do shopping and you may need to help with cleaning every now and then. My daughter used to work there, but she has to move to the Loire with her newlywed husband.'

'Are they nice people?' Karim asked with curiosity and an open mind.

'They are rich Parisians.' Haji shrugged.

Karim went back to his reflective and pensive state and looked at the horizon.

Chapter Five

Another Paris

On a warm, sunny, autumn day in Châtelet in the centre of Paris, the senior women were parading in the private and communal parks and showing off their latest fashion dresses, jewellery, shoes and handbags, while they were being guided by their dogs aimlessly. They seemed happy to follow them to the unknown. Meanwhile younger children were running in the park and creating a loud nuisance to the senior generation whose tranquility was paramount. The younger generation of girls and boys were kissing and hugging under the warm golden rays of the sun.

As everybody in park was busy minding their business, chatting to others, playing with the dogs, or reading a book, eyes turned towards a woman. She was wearing an elegant pink Chanel dress, showing her knees but covering her chest. The dress was a perfect match in colour for her Dolce Gabbana black shoes, but the colour was in contrast to her Hermes crocodile leather handbag. The spectators struggled to figure out the distinctive and familiar person. A huge white Panama hat was covering her face and made her even more of a mystery. She turned to the public with a theatrical move as she took off her Chanel sunglasses and uncovered her face with dark-blue eyes lined with black kohl and mascara-lengthened eyelashes that could be confused with artificial ones. She opened her handbag and took out a small golden mirror to check the accuracy with which she had applied her make-up that took her almost two hours to accomplish, starting from applying the foundation to her sagging face and making balloons to fill her cheeks with air. Nevertheless, she was not satisfied with the results. She walked, preceded by her dog who was trying to set himself free from the imposed restrictive life and the suffocating love from his owner. Sandrine watched her audience from the corner of her eye as she called her dog.

'Lulu, behave.' Her calls were calculated and deliberate to attract the fading attention of her fans. And they were not a success, until an elderly man approached with a calculated and careful move as he came closer to her. He was wearing an Yves Saint Laurent suit and a black hat and holding a mahogany stick. He waved and touched his hat in a gentlemanly way. She missed gentlemanly manners and old-fashioned chivalry.

'Bonjour, madame,' he said.

Sandrine looked at him, thinking perhaps he was an old fan or maybe an admirer. She scanned his body; a wrinkly face told stories of an affluent life, thus she decided to respond in a nasal voice, full of arrogance. 'Bonjour.'

'Do you remember me, madame?'

'No.' Her tone was dismissive.

'I am Albert, probably you do not remember me. I was one of the producers of your film *Joie de Vivre*.'

Her memory took her back to her heydays in the hippy and swinging 1960s when the vedette Sandrine competed with the stars of her day and was the best. The fans flocked to her like butterflies around a flower and she was busy pushing them away those days. It was a discriminate act — princes, sheiks, business men and ordinary people had begged for her company.

'Pardon, I do not remember. You must have changed.' Her comment was rude and insinuated that he had become old.

'I have aged,' he said as he touched his face with the forced acceptance of her remark.

'*Oui,* I can see that.' Her disgusted reply repulsed the poor man who lost interest and desire to chat her up. He nodded and moved on.

Just then Sandrine remembered her lost love who she had met on the set of the *Joie du Vivre* film. Eduard had an average look, not tall, but not short, and slightly chubby for a French man, and softly spoken with a southern France accent. He was a shy cameraman and she was an aspiring vedette. Nevertheless, she tried to make advances towards him. He avoided her. Until he disappeared. She searched for him until she learnt he had emigrated to Quebec and was working at a local TV station. There was no Internet, or an address to post a letter. She sent a few letters to that TV station with no response.

During her younger years, she met many young men who she took a shine to. They were good-looking and rich, but her soul was with Eduard. Many years later, she realised the studios moguls who made a fortune from her had pushed the poor man out to protect her future from a hopeless relationship that might have affected her stardom and alienated her fans. The cinema industry controlled its stars, not as bad as Hollywood, but even so, they did. They would rather she liaised with another star.

She realised poor Eduard loved her, but with persuasion, threats and emotional blackmail in addition to a lucrative contract in Canada, he had deserted her. And the rest is past.

Sandrine never married or had children, having been constantly in fear of spoiling her figure.

She woke up from her daydream when her mobile rang and she struggled to find it, and even with more was the struggle to operate it. She answered in a nervous tone. '*Oui!*'

'*Bonjour*, do you have a moment?' The voice of her building manager was trembling in fear of her. He found her scary.

'*Oui.*'

'I have found someone to manage your apartment.'

'What are his credentials?'

'He has some experience of working in Paris.'

'Is he a Parisian?'

'No, he is Syrian.'

She moved the phone away from her ear as if avoiding contamination by a bug, before she raised her voice to a level that attracted the attention of park dwellers.

'Syrian, *mais non!* Is he a Muslim? Oh no!'

'Madame, be careful. We are living in world of political correctness.'

'I do not care. They are not good. Terrorists. I do not trust them. They do not understand our way of life. They are different.' Her high-pitched tone and derogatory comments turned the heads of the park dwellers.

'Pardon, you have sacked four helpers with different excuses. One was vulgar, another was East European and there were many other reasons. He is perfect for the job because he is skilled in repairing flats. And frankly, no agency wants to deal with you anymore.' He added the last statement after a pause.

'How dare you; I pay generously to your agency.'

'Not recently. You owe two months' fees.'

'Disgusting!' She hung up on the poor man. Her finances had been in tatters since work had dried up and her expenses had spiralled and she had fritted away the rest of her fortune to fix botched plastic surgery in a hopeless attempt to regain her long-lost youth. She needed someone to sort out her flat, her only remaining asset that was falling apart. 'Beggars cannot be choosers. If it has to be a Syrian then it is a Syrian. *Je m'en fou,*' she whispered. Sandrine showed indifference with a Gallic shrug, which attracted even more attention.

Chapter six

East meets West

It was a dry, cold day in early winter. Parisians were shivering as they rushed to catch a bus or the Metro to their warm homes after a long working day.

On the other side of the city, Karim sat on a wooden chair eating with his fellow refugees. Lentil soup had been cooked on an electric stove, hidden from the hotel manager who had warned them about the fire hazard, but hunger has no reasoning. The soup was not only bringing nutrition but warmth to the men's strong bodies that were shivering because of the ailing central heating that had not been functioning for a long time despite their endless pleas to the hotel manager to fix it.

The simple meal laid on a newspaper on the floor consisted of humus, onions and pitta bread. The men tore pieces of bread with their hands and immersed it in the humus, which was floating with cheap olive oil. They were gorging themselves on the food as if they have been in a famine. Having worked hard the whole day and there was nothing else to entertain them during the evening but food. Their budget was tight because of the small amount of money they received from social security. The extra money gained from illegal work would go to their families abroad.

Karim had made some money from cash jobs that he sent regularly to his wife, children and his elderly relatives whenever he could but after an illegal dealer took a big chunk in transaction fees there wasn't much left. He was left with no cash to indulge himself.

Mahmoud, a young man with fair skin and dark hair stood up and addressed his fellow countrymen. 'Come on boys! We are in Paris and Christmas is almost here. Let's go and have some fun. Many French girls are around and we might befriend one or two,' he said in a loud voice.

'*Haram*! We should not disobey God's will. It is adultery,' a middle-aged man replied in an abrupt tone.

Mahmoud ignored him and came close to Karim and tapped him on the shoulder. 'Don't take any notice of him. Come on mate, let's have fun in town,' he whispered.

'No mate. I am a married man,' Karim replied in a shy tone with a friendly smile.

'But you are not dead. God allows us to marry four women.'

'But this not a marriage,' Karim said astonished at his misinterpretation of religious facts.

'Come on. You're a teacher and well educated and you belong to a different generation which I hear is more liberal and open nowadays.'

'Correct, but war and its misery and the way we are treated in the West changed my way of thinking and many others have followed suit. I felt life was miserable, nothing but death and blood. You would think the promised other world and the after-life paradise had perks,' Karim added in an undertone.

'Now, we are here, there is less pressure either social or cultural. We should adopt impartial thinking. They call it individualism,' Mahmoud said pointing at Karim in a preaching manner.

Karim eyes strayed as he tried to hide his internal conflict from the others. 'I think you have a point. We need to promote critical thinking among the younger generation. That's what I used to encourage my pupils to do, then problems started. I mean the war which brought everything to a standstill, including our thinking. Listen. let's have a tour of Paris.' He jumped up from the broken chair and headed to the door.

'People pay small fortunes to visit Paris. We are lucky, it is on our doorstep,' Mahmoud said as he followed and tried to take the credit. 'And free,' Mahmoud added as he came closer to the door.

'I need to relax. I am starting a new job tomorrow.' Karim had cold feet.

'What kind of job?'

'I am not sure. My understanding is that it is looking after the place of a rich Parisian woman's flat in Châtelet.'

'Wow, well to do people. You are not going to work as ...' Mahmoud asked with a tone of suspicion.

Karim's face flushed and his voice became tense. 'I am not a servant, just a manager.'

'Of course you are,' he said and tapped Karim's shoulder to calm him.

They laughed and hugged in a fraternity way as they headed to the door.

'May God forgive you, and now you work as a servant to the infidels,' said the middle aged man.

Karim turned with a jerky movement. 'You are ignorant and could be a fool. If so, why are you living off the infidels and living on the dole?'

The middle aged man was shocked to hear such a statement and he started reciting verses of Quran that Karim will end up in hell with doom and gloom . Mahmoud held Karim's hand. 'Leave him alone. He's in a different world.'

'I am sure he is. But to be honest aren't we all. It is the damn war and it doesn't spare anything, not life or property or people's minds or souls and it distorts their beliefs.' Karim threw his statement while advancing to the door.

They left the flat and emerged into fresh air in a cold Paris. 'We are free,' Karim shouted in the street.

Chapter seven

Clash of Stags

Christmas or Noël as the French call it, was approaching. Paris was glittery with Christmas lights and getting ready for visitors and tourists from everywhere.

The Paris council was on a mission to brighten the city with even more lights. The main target was the Champs-Élysées with lights decorating the elm trees and showing the same glamour of design as a garden that was once laid out by architect André Le Nôtre in 1667. His was an amazing transformation from kitchen garden to state of the art. The shops were stocked with the latest Christmas goods which would make profits for some and bankruptcy for others. The spiritual and religious meaning of the season was substituted with commercial gain. Karim braved the cold wind which was touching his face like a sharp-edged dagger that reminded him of the last cold winter in the camp in Aleppo and in the jungle camp. The feeling of bitter cold would stick on his face forever since it had penetrated the thin sheets of the tent in Aleppo and Calais. The only thing in common there was human degradation to its maximum. But it was nothing in comparison to war austerities from torture and rape to humiliation. He was trying to stay focused, remembering the wise Algerian man's advice — keep calm, avoid direct eye contact, speak only when you are spoken to, she speaks English but may pretend not to and answer you in French despite knowing your limited ability in mastering the language. The flashback of his conversation with Haji went through his mind.

'Who does she think she is, the Queen of England,' Karim said.

'I bet the British monarch is much more modest,' Haji replied with a giggle.

'Really why?'

'She is a diva. That's like French royalty. She married and dated rich and powerful men. I know that kind of French. I can speak like her or even better but she will snub my likes.'

'I am worried, Haji.' Karim's voice was shaky.

'Name God in your next step. Listen, think of your wife and children. You need the money to bring them to Europe and to feed those hungry mouths.'

'I will see them in England.'

'Wherever.'

Karim came back to the real world as he walked towards the Arc de Triomphe. He was hoping to walk to Châtelet, to save the Metro fares and buy ingredients for a simple meal.

While he was in his own bubble, he felt a blow to his shoulder that made him stop and lose his balance. He turned to face the angry facial expressions of a young man. Karim realised that he had knocked into the young man by mistake. '*Pardon,*' Karim said in broken French.

The young man got up and came towards Karim shouting and swearing in French. He did not listen to Karim's apology. This made him even more aggressive and he pushed Karim to the ground. Then, out of nowhere, a passer-by tried to resolve the conflict, but the aggressive man would not listen to reason from Karim or others.

The police came and they listened to the other guy in French while Karim tried to explain in his modest English and poor French without success. Some of the passers-by tried to explain to the police that they had witnessed Karim's confusion. The police asked Karim to produce his identity documents. Luckily, he was in the habit of carrying them in Syria when he was out, having had been checked regularly at army points, where they hunted for deserters or if he was accosted by the insurgents who were on a mission to screen those loyal to their cause from the non. Finally, the police were convinced that there was no base to make a case against Karim. Karim wiped his bruises with a tissue given to him by a young woman who was talking on his behalf, and advocating for him over the unpleasant incident.

She tapped his shoulder and spoke in reasonably good English. 'Do not worry. Not all of us are like that.'

He thanked her and asked for directions to Châtelet. Karim regretted his plan to save money that ended up with a drama. He would have had done better with the Metro. According to his calculations, he would have had enough time to walk. But not any more after the unpleasant, unplanned confrontation; he would be late for his job interview. Haji's warning resonated in his ears, "Never upset the diva. The French people like their appointments to be respected." To Karim, it was an achievable task. It was no surprise to him, he was used to making instant decisions, running from air raids, escaping tanks or intelligence spies. It was about his everyday bread and butter back home.

It was common sense to use the Metro. He advanced to Champs-Élysées-Clemenceau Metro Station, and descended the escalator in a remarkable haste, mortified about the witch that the agent had hinted was to be his new employer. He got on the first train with a lot of hesitation and anxiety. He was heading in the right direction, wasn't he? He started counting stations with a pounding heart. He watched the faces of the

Parisians as they avoided each other. He was mesmerised by their elegance and smartphones. One woman was wearing a wintery flowery manteau and fixing her make-up while looking in her mirror. A middle-aged man wearing a designer suit was eyeing a young girl with tight jeans. It brought a smile to her face. She had blue eyes and shiny brunette hair. Karim wondered if those people were happy or felt miserable like him. 'At least they have no war,' he mumbled. His thoughts took him back to his wife and children as he dreamt of a reunion. Before he woke up from his absent-minded state, he heard the announcement for Châtelet that made him rush to the door. He pushed the standing passengers, but it was too late. The door shut firmly. Karim swore in Arabic to the surprise of some and discontent of others. He looked at the map on his mobile. The next stop was Hôtel de Ville. Well, he should not get too grumpy. 'I can walk,' he muttered. He ascended the escalators and once he was on the street the chilly breeze was sharp and cut into his bare face. Thinking it was protected by his greyish beard was a fallacy. The Hôtel de Ville struck him with its fine Belle Époque architecture. He was curious to know more about the building and he tried to use a search engine to find out. His limited Internet data ran out. *I will look it up later.* He walked north following the map in haste indifferent to the magnificent Parisian architecture around him. He followed the correct directions as he remembered his journey from Syria to France. The majority of it was on foot. Then he came face to face with the Châtelet theatre in all its magnificent with its sumptuous facade. He walked for a few more minutes in search of Rue Bertin Poirée. There was a change in the architecture; it was elegant but more modern. Then he spotted the building — modest in comparison to some Parisian architecture but still outstanding. Karim looked for the flat number, but all he found was the name Sandrine La Croix. It looked like an advertisement for a film. He rang the bell and waited. After a long wait of ten minutes that seemed forever, he wanted to leave but the image of his children bombarded him. Were they alive or dead, hungry or not? The dream of securing his residency in the UK with his children and wife, or even in France took him away on a mental journey. He woke up when a voice that sounded as if it was from another era spoke.

'*Bonjour, oui?*'

'*Bonjour.* I am Karim,' he stammered with anxiety.

'*Oui* Karim?'

'I am the new helper.' He swallowed his pride, as he thought to himself, *I am just a servant.*

The voice changed to English. 'Come in.' The gate opened by remote. The hall was filled with replicas of Rodin's statues, but it was chilly and Karim felt even colder. He knew the flat number but became confused because of his huge anxiety. Was it number one or two? Then he remembered to look at his messages from Haji. It was number two. He took the stairs. He knocked on the door. Not long after the door opened. A middle-aged servant spoke in a broken French. 'Madame is waiting.' She came right to the point and didn't ask him to identify himself before she ushered him to the lounge. It was very grand. He was gobsmacked by the grandiose furniture, paintings and statues. What grasped his attention was the photos of a pretty woman. She was very beautiful, a brunette with blue eyes and a slender figure. He stopped before the photo of a naked woman. He felt his body calling, he had not been in the company of a woman since leaving his wife. He felt his private parts with embarrassment. And to his shame he heard a loud voice speak. '*Les amants.*'

Karim turned to see an old pale woman, her face was covered with layers of make-up that she had probably spent a good many hours applying to try to achieve a younger look by hiding facial lines that told years of stories. Her figure was slim and her slender legs were covered by a long dress that hid the saggy folds of skin. She was lying in the lounger, relaxing. She pointed at him. 'Approach *moi*,' she said. Karim came closer. She continued addressing him in English. Deep down she was flattered. She had picked up his excitement when he'd seen the naked photo of her. Such reactions were non-existent from men nowadays.

'You need to take your orders from me mostly. I am the mistress and you may need to take a few from the housekeeper. Besides the shopping, you may have to help with cleaning and repairs. I was told that you are skilled in that domain.' Her speech came like bullets showered from the gun of a confident army officer in the Syrian Army or an IS fighter.

He wanted to tell her that he was an academic, but he bit the bullet as Haji had taught him, do he didn't make his mistress feel that he was above her intellectually. '*D'accord*,' he replied to make her feel that he could communicate according to Haji's instructions.

She rang the golden bell on the Louis XIV marble table. The housekeeper appeared. '*Oui*, madame.' Sandrine asked her to accompany him to the door by waving her hand towards the door without the slightest eye contact. Karim felt the humiliation bone-deep. He heard a voice that came like thunder from the slim, old, weak body. 'Stop,' she said. 'You have to walk the dog too.' She started petting her Chihuahua as Karim tried relentlessly to distract the dog from licking his feet.

For Karim, it was the last straw. 'I do not like dogs to come near me,' he exploded as he moved away from the dog.

'Why? They are friendly.' She changed her tone to a cold and sarcastic.

'I cannot like them. I pray and I have to cleanse.'

'I am doing business with you, no need to be politically correct.'

'Okay, madame, my service is not at your disposal,' Karim said in a confident tone.

'Up to you.' She turned her face away with apparent indifference.

He left by the main door much to the housekeeper's astonishment.

Sandrine turned and looked at her face in the mirror. She didn't like what she saw. *'Mon Dieu!'* Then she started talking to herself and counting how many wrinkles she had. *Why do I have to be rude to others? All my nearest and dearest have deserted me. Now, there is another one to cross off my list.* She was aware that her abrasive behaviour and manners never discriminated or saved any of her family, friends or acquaintances. Yes, she was sceptical about Karim's background. He was a refugee — Arab, Muslim. One character was enough for her to worry about, let alone the three. But it was his misfortune to be displaced from his native country. She recalled her desperate attempt to break through to Hollywood in the 1960s with her limited English, and no friends; however, she was equipped with a modest name in France and her gorgeous looks and body. She felt guilty and shouted before she threw an ashtray which smashed on the floor.

The housekeeper was used to it. 'Here we go again, same old, same old,' she said.

A trailer of her losses from family members to lovers and husbands was playing in Sandrine's mind. Alas!

Chapter Eight

Getting out of Hell

Aleppo is the old crossroads city famed for its monopoly between East and West, having been inhabited since the sixth millennium. The Citadel had stood intact against invaders, wars, anarchy and earthquakes since the twelfth century, but the city was struggling with the bombing from different unknown parties and the confusion of the civilian victims running from their destroyed houses to the relative safety of the refugee camps around the city or even further to the Turkish border, if they were lucky enough to make it. They could not distinguish between an enemy and a friend. They lost count of the planes and the artillery bombing which came from the Syrian Government, the Russians, the Americans, Iran or Turkey. It did not matter who. The end result was one — death and destruction. Aleppo had been the target of the fighting parties because of its strategic position and the attraction of merchants in the past and war planes in the present.

Fadwa teamed up with her family and parents to escape the hell in the city which also followed them to the refugee camps next to the Turkish border. The journey was difficult and she lost her one-year-old nephew who died from severe diarrhoea. Infectious diseases were rife with the lack of the basic healthcare and hygiene among the refugees. The journey took a few days by bus, hitchhiking and walking in the freezing winter. Snow fell for the first time in a few years.

The thin textile of the tents did not protect them from the cold weather. Turkish refugee camps were flooded with Syrian refugees numbering from two to four million, and much beyond the capacity of a country with limited resources. Fadwa followed her brother and his family, hoping to reach the Turkish territories, aspiring to gain asylum and have a better chance to join Karim and start a new life in peace abroad. She hugged her children Ahmed and Randa to protect them from cold chilly, freezing wind and most of all, fear of the unknown. Her thoughts were fixated on living or dying together. Her mother stayed behind with her father who begged her to leave with her brother to join her husband in Europe at a later stage. Her mother's wise words resonated in her ear, "Your future is with your husband and family. We will manage." The echo of her mother's words had engulfed her with fear *and* guilt as she left her parents to the unknown.

The group aimed to get to Suruc camp behind the Turkish border where it was rumoured there was faster processing of asylum applications. This was the move that cost them the life of her nephew. This tormented her day and night. What if she lost her children on the way out? She woke after a restless night and glanced at the snow covering the tent like a white coat. The refugees dreaded needing to use the toilet because there wasn't one. Fadwa had hidden under her clothes what was left of her family paperwork as Karim had instructed her to do. Some were hidden in the most private part of her body. She was not willing to reveal the papers to the Syrian soldiers who had searched them and were sniffing through the fugitive crowds in search of young men who were suspected to be Islamic State fighters or belonged to the Al-Nusra Front or the

Fertile Crescent fighters. Different names, but Fadwa believed that they had the same goal. The opposite side of the conflict fighters were not any kinder to her or her fellow fleeing Syrian citizens.

'Hey you, woman. Do you carry American dollars?' A young Syrian solider hissed in her ear in a jovial tone.

'We are poor. We have nothing.' She pointed at her body, saying that she had nothing to declare.

'But you have a lot to give.' He came very close to touching her body with his private parts. She loathed his smell especially his breath and tried to get away when he cornered her. His unmet sexual need has converted to anger and vile aggression.

'Let's search you,' he said in a sharp angry tone.

Fadwa tried to avoid the pitfall and wanted to calm him down using Delilah's charm by acting the submissive female and talking in a seductive tone. 'You are a nice man and we have lost our livelihood. You have a family. I am like your sister. Please let me and my children pass. May God bless you and guard you.' Her soft voice worked wonders on the deprived solider who had been in the war zone for as long as he could remember and he had virtually lost the memory and meaning of a family. He hadn't been in touch with a women properly for a long while. He examined the paperwork she showed him and ushered her past. Her calmness worked wonders and she burst into tears as she held her children tight, screaming at them, yet more at herself. The journey was long and hard, but her determination was strong as was her survival instinct. It took her a few days to reach her destination. On the way she lost her brother's family when they were stopped and detained by the Syrian authorities. She had to pretend that she had no connection to them and continue her journey. Her mind shut down on everything. *Nothing but myself, my children and Karim.* Survival of the fittest.

The walk to the alleged freedom was hard and paved with sweat and blood. Fadwa looked back and was sad. *Will I be able to forget my birthplace. I hate it now but I will miss it later.* She held tightly to her children as she walked on the slippery ground covered with black ice, over the footprints of many refugees before. She felt the chill deep down in her bones, not only the cold weather but also the fear of the unknown to come. She woke up from her daydream and flashbacks to the sound of the sirens announcing a raid but where could they hide?

Chapter Nine

Tomorrow is Another World

Paris' chilly dry winter wind caused the elegant Parisians to get out their designer coats from their wardrobes — brand names ranging from the Chanel in Place Vendôme to Primark in Saint-Denis. Elegance comes first, regardless of the budget. Some took hours of preparations before heading to the Metro to get to work or commuting by Vélib bikes, for those encouraged by the government to diminish car use and reduce pollution. A young girl with high heels and full make-up was steering her bike skillfully towards the Metro station. Others were having coffee and fresh croissant at the local café before heading to a tough working day.

The other Paris is a completely different place. In Châtelet, Sandrine woke up at nine a.m. to the noise of her barking dog. She rang the golden bell next to her bed. The maid deliberately ignored her ever-demanding, never-pleased, always-complaining mistress. 'Where are you? You pig,' Sandrine shouted.

The maid entered with a red face resembling an erupting volcano and responded fiercely to Sandrine's inappropriate remark. She advanced on Sandrine's bed. Sandrine pushed herself to the far edge. The dog was barking at the maid, but the maid wouldn't budge. 'I am fed up with you, your voice, your rudeness, your arrogance and your face too,' she spat.

'How dare you talk to me like this.' Sandrine's tone was filled with intimidation.

'How dare you to call me pig.'

'You did not respond to me.'

'So what, I have been cleaning your shit. You dirty pig.'

'You ignorant Bulgarian, don't you know who I am?'

'You were an actress who made her name because of her body, but that is finished, long gone.' The maid took off her apron and threw it at Sandrine's face. 'You know what, you sort yourself out and I feel sorry for anyone who associates with you.' The maid left swearing in her native tongue.

Sandrine heard the door slam. She made sure the maid had left before she shouted, 'Bulgarian bitch, go back home.' She got up and walked to the adjacent silvery mirror hanging on the wall of the living room. 'I am ugly. Look at the wrinkles. Is that the beautiful Sandrine who men once loved. They used to bathed my feet with Champagne. Yes, once upon a time.' She burst into tears. No family, no friends, no work, no good looks. Nothing but those wrinkles to keep her company and it was difficult to soften them with all the plastic surgery and Botox in the world. She picked up the gilded landline phone and dialled.

A voice spoke. '*Oui* Mademoiselle La Croix?'

'I want a housekeeper, a maid, a helper, whatever.'

'What happened, we have just got you one?'

'I sacked her.'

'Impossible, after only three weeks.'

Sandrine raised her voice in agitation. 'She was useless. I want another one.'

'Sorry, no one wants to work for you. We cannot afford the government clamp down on bullying and abuse at work.'

'You are useless!' She hung up. O*h that Muslim boy. He is a refugee and must be desperate to earn a living.* She searched her old-fashioned address book that was dotted with numbers.

She remembered François has made a note of Karim's phone number. *Aha, I need to swallow my pride and call him.* She dialled the number.

'Allo?' The voice on the other end was strong, masculine and assertive and it moved something inside her. 'Yes, how can I help you?'

'Is that Karim?'

Yes, it is.'

'Sandrine La Croix.'

'Yes?'

'What do you mean, yes?' she replied in fierce English heavily accented with French.

'What do you want?'

'Well. Ha! Ha!' She was hesitant to talk as she tried to swallow her pride and she produced a big phew sound.

'Out with it woman.'

His angry tone irritated her. 'How dare to address me like that, you … you insignificant thing.' Her arrogant tone replaced the previous sheepish one.

'What do you want?'

'I am Sandrine La Croix and in my culture men respect women.'

'You need to respect someone for them to respect you,' he replied with confidence.

'You arrogant Arab!'

'If I am arrogant what are you then? You are a senior woman and in my culture we respect women, particularly the older ones, even those with a foul mouth.'

The word senior was a dagger in her heart. Her narcissistic personality drove her to the edge. 'I do not need you. Go to hell. Back to your country. You are a backward Muslim.' She hung up swearing and poured a glass of Bordeaux wine that she downed immediately. *'Merde!* My therapist told me my impulsive behaviour is part of my psychopathic personality. So, I sacked her. I am going to sack everyone. I am alone now.'

Chapter ten

Hopes and Aspirations

Karim had always been determined to pursue his dream and reach his target of heading to England. He was learning English, using all the free apps available in the hope of reaching his dreamland and eventually reuniting with his family. Nonetheless, Haji convinced him to try to learn French. He told him once that this was the problem with immigrants, including his parents. There was free tuition in French offered by the government but immigrants do not take what is on offer to ameliorate their lives.

He had been touring Paris from the north to the south, and east to west, asking and begging at times for a job so that he could raise a decent sum of money to support his family back at the refugee camp and his parents who stayed behind in Aleppo, let alone the outstanding costs of smuggling himself and his family to the UK. He tried cleaning jobs, chewing his pride to accept any or whatever job, listening to his mentor Haji and hanging on his recommendations.

The pay was too low and he was exploited like a slave to work for cash in his hand. The benefit allocated by social security hardly supported his food shopping and rent. He had to live in expensive Paris where were more work opportunities were available than outside it.

He was playing with his mobile when Saad, a young Algerian he had worked asked him what he was doing.

'What are you up to?'

'I need to polish my English.'

'Listen, young man. Come down to earth and stop dreaming. Many guys I knew went to sea and never came back on either shore. You cannot live in La La land forever.'

'Please do not make my dream hit the rocks on a turbulent shore. It is all that I am living for.'

'You could be a naturalised French citizen and it would be easier to move around and be treated like a human.'

Saad's words resonated in Karim's mind as he strolled along the Seine River which was his best form of escapism. He walked by the shore near the Pont Neuf and watched the soft waves, initiated by the noisy tourists boats and disturbing the serenity of the eternal river. He enjoyed the Rive Gauche on Saturdays and walking to the antique bookseller's stalls. He went there whenever he had time to spare when he was out of work.

On Sundays, he enjoyed the tranquility that took him back to his birth place Aleppo. To the citadel, the streets and the market where he grew up, and walked and talked. He found freedom from his jam-packed room that he shared with other fellow countrymen, and two or three extras when they could not turn down an unannounced guest.

Occasionally, he tried to find time for himself without having to push unnecessary compliments on a stranger or praising someone who pretended to own the earth and France yet was surviving on a pittance from social security and criticised his way of living when he associated with other immigrants. His thoughts strayed to his parents, his wife and children and at times to a more practical plan about how to reach England with his family. The dream kept him going.

He woke up to the phone ringing tone of Arabic music and came back to the bitter reality of life. He looked at the screen which showed an unidentified caller.

He pressed the response button and heard a harsh, coarse voice, exhausted from shouting and smoking. Karim was mortified. Had something bad happened to his family? Every phone call was an alarm to death or destruction. His hands were shaking; he could hardly hold the mobile. The voice hit his ears like thunder. '*Salaam alaykum,*' Karim answered in a faint voice.

'*Alaykum salaam.* Is this Karim?'

'Yes.'

'My name is Mahmoud and I am from the refugee camp.' The last few words landed like someone had struck his head.

'Nice to know you.' The pause seemed to Karim to go on for ages.

'There is someone who wants to talk to you.'

'Who is that?'

'Wait a minute.' Mahmood's voice disappeared among the noise of people who were calling and making disgruntled noises and protesting. Then a familiar voice spoke.

'Karim darling, where are you?'

'Fadwa. How are you? How are the children?'

'They are fine. We have reached Suruc camp in Turkey. They say it is easier to get United Nations recognition there and we could get reunited with you.'

'Of course darling. And the children?'

'They are fine. Dying to see you.'

'So am I.'

'How are your parents?'

'They declined to join us and went to the village to stay with their extended family. The journey would have been too much for them; I wanted them to accompany us but they refused. My aunts are stuck in Lebanon and I cannot join them. Syrians are banned from entering Lebanon.'

'The situation is dire.' Karim uttered his words with a big sigh in anticipation of hearing bad news.

'Much worse than you think.' Fadwa followed her comment with weeping noises. She paused. 'Mahmoud wants to talk to you,' she added. She handed him the smartphone.

'*Salaam* again. I can see you want to get your family out.'

'Of course I do.'

'Do you want them to go to France?'

'I would rather the UK.'

'Well, the cost is double around 20,000 US dollars with a reduced commission.'

'It is too much.'

'I swear with my kids that it costs more. The amount can hardly cover your wife let alone your grown-up children from France to England. I am sure you are aware of that.' Mahmoud handed the mobile phone to Fadwa, knowing that one tear from her hazel eyes was worth more than the sum he suggested to Karim.

'I will do anything to see you. Please help,' she said before her voice broke and she spluttered.

All of a sudden a huge bang noise deafened Karim's ears.

'Hello Fadwa, Fadwa, talk to me,' Karim screamed. But her voice disappeared without trace.

'When will we meet again?' he mumbled.

Chapter eleven

Clash of the Mountains

The Parisian winter was harsh. Cold whistling drafts penetrated the gentle Parisian architecture, and the temperature was reduced even further with mini draughts blowing between the buildings.

It was business as usual as it had always been. People were moving in and out of the Metro stations, along the roads and into buildings, minding their own business careless of their surroundings.

On the other side, it was a different Paris. Rich affluent Parisians were hanging out in Saint-Germain-des-Prés boutiques. Posh women wearing Lanvin and Chanel woollen coats with matching designer hats paraded in the shops, buying luxuries after waking up late, following a boozy Champagne night in a prestigious nightclub or hotel.

Sandrine suffered broken sleep or perhaps more a lack of it as far as she could remember. It has been caused by her excessive alcohol intake, old age and anxiety. Waking up late was not an option. She browsed shop windows, stopping at Louis Vuitton, where she examined the latest fashion handbags and wondered about adding one to her large collection. She couldn't help her jaw dropping as she looked at the price tag which was far beyond her means. Her roles in films had dried up. There were no agents who could find her a role because she reduced other actors to tears by her rudeness or demanding roles younger than her real age. Her pride and joy, had been when she was a double César award winner, but she was a star and a diva and less of an actor. César is the French equivalent of the American Oscars. No company wanted her to endorse their cosmetics or accessory products; she'd been dropped after her racially aggressive messages to the government through the French media, when she incited hatred against immigrants who were not affiliated to French culture. She maintained that her main goal was preserving the French way of life and culture. Others thought she was blinded by racism, but many were in agreement with her.

It was lunchtime and Sandrine felt the thirst for a drink before hunger after an aimless tour window shopping with no spare cash. She went to a glamorous brasserie called Les Deux Magots where the high-heeled Parisians and some well to do foreigners paraded in that glamorous, well sought after area. Sandrine felt frustration at the social decline that Saint-Germain-des-Prés had been undergoing in the last few years. It was no longer a magnet for glamorous people who used to frequent it. Still she felt the need for a drink. She walked fast pulling her poor Chihuahua dog who was barking aggressively, but Sandrine did not respond to his begging to reduce her pace until she dashed into the café. It looked strange inside. She had not been out of her flat for as long as she could remember. She sucked in her lips in disapproval of the decor.

She went straight to the bar and asked the young blond barman to serve her a glass of Champagne. She would have to restrict her food intake and replace it with drinks. The barman did not recognise her. *How could you not know a vedette like me.*

The young blond guy looked at her with amusement when she raised her voice. *'Je suis la grande damme. Vous êtes fou?'* Her voice grew louder and louder under the influence of alcohol on an empty stomach.

Her offending remarks reached the young man ears like an electric shock and before he reacted, despite being trained to cope with rude-rich customers, he was about to respond when Paul, who was sixty-something barged in to stop the young man from uttering an inappropriate comment. He held Sandrine's soft hand and planted a kiss on it with a bow as he addressed her like he was reciting a poem. 'Mademoiselle Sandrine, what a pleasure meeting you.'

'What is wrong with your staff? Don't you train them?' she asked in a theatrical manner resembling the Queen of France.

'Ignorance mam, it is pure ignorance. The younger generation have no culture. Who does not know Sandrine La Croix?'

Sandrine ego was flattered despite the protest on the face of the young waiter and the barking dog noise. She took the glass of Champagne and downed it happily. Paul had upgraded it to Dom Perignon. She paused in a theatrical gesture, as if she was on the stage of the La Comédie Française receiving warm applause. Paul wanted to strike while the iron was hot and to create publicity for his glamour-fading restaurant.

'Mam, I saw you at the theatre, you were acting in a Mollier production.'

'Oui. Have I worked in theatre?' The alcohol had hit her head directly via an empty stomach. She wanted to have her moment of fame.

'You were great.'

'Merci.' She paraded on the bar floor emulating a theatre act as she recalled the days of glory and how she had proved to the producers that she was a serious actor, playing with the La Comédie Française, defying the critique whose reviews said she was a cheap, porno cinema star.

'A diva, is that what you think I am?' she'd said to her agent to make him consider her seriously as a theatre actress at the advanced age of her career.

Paul brought her back to the real world. 'Mam, shall we offer you a better champagne?'

'No need; this is not too bad after all.' She uttered her words incoherently after becoming tipsy.

'It's on the house,' he replied.

'*Merci.*' In her prime days, she had never paid at Maxim's or at any other Michelin star restaurants.

Things had changed since wrinkles crept on to her pretty face despite a few hopeless botched plastic surgeries and endless Botox injections.

The free drinks flew and before long Sandrine was drunk and chasing young male customers, picking the well-dressed and well-presented ones to the embarrassment of the restaurant's management and their partners. Paul realised the mistake of offering her the free alcohol and the result was dire. The older generation of the restaurant customers realised who she was and they were entertained by a once-upon-a-time star. She was so tipsy that her steps were unbalanced in her stilettos designed by Francesco Russo. She defied her doctor's advice; he had warned her about possible bone fracture owing to malnutrition and excessive alcohol consumption. There was a high risk to her fragile bones. Sandrine moved elegantly to the tango music played by Paul to revive her part in the 1960s famous dance scene in the film *Les Étrangers* shot in Argentina. She approached a table where a handsome young man wearing a blue Saville Row suit that matched his blue eyes and complimented his red hair, was sitting. He was shy, but she was not after a few drinks on an empty stomach. She paused like the legendary French actress Sarah Bernhardt picking her lovers, and asked him to dance with her without uttering a word but using eye contact in the old-fashioned way. She added to his embarrassment and shyness, but regardless he stood up without having received permission from his female partner who gulped her Bordeaux glass of wine with evident dismay. Sandrine grabbed the young man and held his strong well-toned muscly body close to her floppy, weak and wasted one. To her surprise, he was an expert Tango dancer and he held her tight while she was intoxicated with alcohol and unsteady on her high heels despite her lightweight body. She managed to manoeuvre his fast, strong and determined swings that took her back to those days when she danced with famous dancers on and off screen and stage. The cameras turned on but not the old film ones but the ones from the smartphones with flashing that made her revisit her studio heydays. Alcohol and joy made her lose control and become direct to the shy young man.

'What is your name?'

'Gerard.'

'Nice name. What do you do for living?'

'I'm a banker.'

'I thought so.'

'Is she your girlfriend?' Sandrine threw a black look at the poor girlfriend.

'Yes.'

She straightened her body and became less close to him as sign of respect.

'What do you do for living?' he asked her.

The question fell like a thunder overhead. She stopped. 'Don't you watch films? I am Sandrine the big star of France and Hollywood. How ignorant the younger generation is.' Her look of disgust and disrespect hit him like a dart. He loosened his grip on her petit body.

Oh no, again I have made a mess, merde.' She started to lose her control and after pushing the young man away she shouted, 'Go away.' Her shouts filled the place and she fell to the floor. The lights dimmed; the faces were unclear. Nothing but flashes from the restaurant clients' smartphones. They were flashes that she had craved for a long time but for the wrong reason.

Chapter twelve

Leaving Paradise

The cold season arrived early to Paris. Karim got a job at the meat market at Rue de la Roquette. The pay was cash in hand. The owner was a sixty-something Corsican who took huge pride in his origin. Despite the disgracefully low wages Karim worked like a dog up to eighteen hours a day sometimes. He woke early at four in the morning and took two early buses to Rue de la Roquette where he was greeted by his boss' demands, orders and at times swear words. He put up with all the insults patiently to raise money to support his family in exile. Money was tight and the food rations offered by the Red Cross were barely sufficient to keep them going in the cold weather.

But most of all, he wanted to reunite with his wife and children and cover the hefty cost of smuggling them to Europe. His thoughts wandered between the wise advice of Haji who asked him to save as much as possible to cover a very expensive journey, preferably with legal means, and if the worst came to the worst, he would pay smugglers to take a risky route to freedom. He dismissed the latter, when he remembered to his horror how he had walked for days trans-Europe crossing the borders from Turkey and Eastern Europe and suffering the humiliation. He loathed and despised many of the citizens of those countries along the way. He'd spent days without having a shower as he looked for a piece of dry bread to satisfy his hunger.

He woke from his day dream/nightmare to the shouting of his rough boss telling him to focus on work or he would cut his fingers accidentally with the electric saw. Karim gave his full attention to his work and put the abuse and humiliation aside until one day when he got fed up with the assistant who called him backward and stupid after Karim muddled an order. Consequently, there was an argument that ended up in a fight.

'Go back home,' the French assistant shouted in loud voice, *'Rentrez chez vous.'* Karim could not digest this insult. *Go back where? I have nowhere to go to.* The boss came in and tried to de-escalate the situation. He could well have felt the persecution because he was a Corsican who had been accused of terrorism during the 1970s and 1980s when his country was striving for independence from France.

He pushed the assistant and spoke loudly in a strong Corsican accent. 'Leave him alone. This is my shop and if you don't like it leave.' Karim was hardly in control of the sharp butcher's knife as he clutched it with his shaky hand. The Corsican approached him and took the lethal object from his hand. 'Son, life is hard and I have been through a lot of shit but never like yours.'

'I am fed up with being told I don't belong here. I was told the same in my native Aleppo, then Damascus, Turkey, Hungry, Italy and now France.' Karim burst into tears.

The old man hugged him and Karim was overwhelmed by the unusual kindness. 'You are the manager now,' the Corsican boss whispered in his ear. Karim was happy, almost hitting the roof at the prospect of receiving higher pay. He would be able to save money. Then the old man extended his generosity. 'Where do you live?'

'Belleville.'
'Sharing a flat?'
'Actually, a room monsieur.'
'And you pay rent, I understand.'
'Of course.'
'You can stay in the room above the shop and save yourself the rent.'

Karim was over the moon. He could have jumped from the roof. With all those concessions and freebies he would be able to save money to send to his family. He went into a daydream.

Chapter thirteen

The Fall from Grace

Sandrine's dog was barking aggressively at the building concierge whose regular complaints about the undisciplined and spoilt dog's behaviour were ignored by Sandrine.

As usual, the mail delivery went through the door slot; a pile of letters and leaflets that had no interest for her. Sandrine continued to live the old-era life. Email and social media were out of her reach. Newspapers, magazines and TV were her main source of information, if she could focus on reading the articles. Sandrine woke up with a heavy head from the hangover preceded by a blackout from the heavy drinking session the night before. With her fuzzy head she could not precisely recall what had taken place the night before. Her memory was hazy about what she'd done at the restaurant. Yet she knew she had drunk to excess and listened to Tango music with a handsome young man. But what else? She pulled the golden bell and shook it violently. When she received no response, she started shouting, but there was still no response. Regardless, she continued shouting until she remembered that she has sacked her maid and the Syrian guy respectively. She pulled her fragile old body upright with difficulty as she felt aches and pains all over her body. It took her ages to walk to the door with the impact of seventy-something years on her weak body. Nevertheless, her mind's sharpness never betrayed her. She picked up a bundle of magazines *Le Matin, Point de Vue, Elle* and *Femme Actuelle*. She dragged her body to the kitchen, where her half asleep eyes searched for the coffee percolator. She chased the caffeine shot like chasing a mirage in the middle of the desert.

Having been reliant on her maid, she had no knowledge about her kitchen or its utensils. She opened the cabinet and a coffee pot fell to the ground. She followed it, diving to the marble floor where she burst into tears. *What a life I have got myself to. No friends, no family.* It was a trial. How she had struggled and fought tooth and nail to become the top diva of the Francophone world media. She got up and put the cups in place. The kitchen sink was full of dirty cups, plates and cutlery. She spotted the percolator with triumph but struggled to find the coffee beans. Then she opened the fridge and found them. The smell of coffee revived her. It was a sense of achievement to make a cup of coffee, having not entered the kitchen for a while. She walked to the living room and placed her hot cup on the gilded coffee table.

The dog stopped barking and protesting about her tears that poured heavily. 'What a miserable lonely life,' she mumbled.

After few sips of her strong bitter coffee, her dog began barking in response to her cry of, *'Mon Dieu!'* The magazine fell from her trembling hands. She looked at the photos. *'Dégueulasse!'* The paparazzi had brought her back to fame but for the wrong reason. She turned the pages hurriedly and read the headlines: *Is She Sane? Wants to be Young. Fall from Grace.* The headlines were overwhelming. She was bemused with the fast travel of news via social media and the mobile phone to the media. In her day it used to take a lot of time and organization to get to the media. And she had got away with a lot. The producers and cinema moguls would have negotiated a decent exit from such an embarrassment with the media. It was a new different age.

While she was thinking aloud, the phone rang and brought her back to earth. Sandrine approached the phone but could not touch it. *What will it be next?* She braved it and picked it up.

'*Allo.*'

'*Bonjour,* I am Fred from your agency.'

'Yes?'

'Madame. We need to discuss what happened yesterday.'

'What do you mean?'

'I am afraid we cannot represent you anymore.'

'What do you mean? I was promised a TV role.'

'I am sorry.'

'Fuck off. *Merde!* Shit! She threw the phone on the marble floor.

Pourquoi? Why does everything have to go wrong for me? Why can't I get it right? She felt the need to be swallowed by the ground and never exist.

Sandrine sat on the cool floor and wept accompanied by her dog who appeared to pity her misfortune. She could have done better without her infamous stand at the restaurant. 'Maid!' she cried but there was no answer except the barking of her dog. 'Just me and you, alone.' She caressed her dog who was confused by her mood changes.

Chapter fourteen

Lost Everything

Days went by and Karim was working like a dog. His days were interwoven with nights. Work and work was all that Karim had in his life. In the morning he headed to the meat market at six and worked all day long until the market closed around seven in the evening. He also managed to find cleaning jobs at some Parisian households. Cleaning bathrooms and toilets was the hardest part of the job. He succeeded in keeping this secret from his fellow countrymen and his boss, to save him losing face.

He disclosed what he was doing in confidence to his trustworthy friend Haji when the latter offered him the opportunity to work. 'I can cope with butchery work, but cleaning, it is very difficult.'

'You know very well that you do not have the licence to work in France. It has to be under the table kind of work. But you need the money to reunite with your family.'

'And support the rest living in Syria,' Karim added.

'Exactly. You need a small fortune, even the average working French person could not afford.'

Karim came back to real life when his boss ushered him into to his office. He spoke in broken English with his heavy Corsican dialect. His French was no better than Karim's. He needed to use his hands very often. 'Listen Karim, your French has improved and you speak it better than me. Since I have sacked the deputy manager, I want you to take over a more responsible role.'

Karim was taken by surprise. 'Do you mean it, you like my work and my French is good?'

'*Oui* Monsieur. You have coped tremendously in the last eight months. Your popularity in the market is huge. At times, I fear that you are going to be too well known and you will leave me.'

'Never sir, you are kind to me.' Karim knew that his boss could not further his career because he had no work permit. His salary had gone up, but it was a pittance compared to his French counterparts'. Nevertheless, his pay was tax free and that would allow him to save more money.

Besides eating leftovers, at times he treated himself to a cheap cut of meat preferably halal, which catered for the large Muslim community in Paris. He also relied on pulses, bread and vegetables, which saved him a lot. Fruit was a treat. His saving plan secured him a reasonable sum of money that he deposited with Haji for a rainy day. Karim was counting the money: one, two, three, four and finally five thousand euros. He was counting the pennies and getting ready to pay a smuggler to bring his wife and children to France. Britain was on the back-burner, but it was always the final target. While he was thinking his ex-roommate Souhaib attracted his attention as they were catching up in an Algerian café. 'Hey, come back to earth.'

'Sorry, just thinking about my family.'

'Don't we all.'

'I want to confide in you.'

'By all means.'

'I've saved some cash.'

Souhaib's eyes radiated excitement and some envy. 'How much?' he asked.

Karim felt an unpleasant vibe and was hesitant to say but succumbed to his friend's insistence.

'Around five thousand euros.'

Souhaib opened his mouth wide. 'Make sure not to deposit it in the bank. Keep them somewhere safe.' He scanned the corners of the small-cramped cafe.

'Aren't banks safe?' Karim asked.

'Maybe you need help to bring the family.' Souhaib picked up the desperation on Karim's face.

'Oh, it is a dream,' Karim said and looked at the ceiling.

'I know someone who can help you.'

'Who is he?'

'He is a reliable Syrian guy, almost a cousin. He came from my village and would not cheat me.'

'Can he bring my family to France?' Karim interrupted him with his desperate excitement.

'I am sure he could. I can fix an appointment with him for you.'

Karim looked in the horizon with a fearful look. 'Why not.'

Chapter fifteen

Hard Times

Sandrine spent a great deal of time moving between mental health institutions in Paris, seeking help from the most prominent psychiatrists and psychologists. However, after a while she sacked them one after the other.

'Madame, I cannot change your personality component,' she recalled a top Parisian psychiatrist daring to tell her. She was furious at his remark and never saw him again.

She was in and out of the Clinique du Château de Garches Nightingale on the outskirts of Paris anonymously. But alas, the media found out. *The 1960s Icon is going Mad,* said the headlines.

The nurses tried to hide the magazines and newspapers and even censored the TV programmes on TF1, TF2 and even TV5. She was left to watch her old films, and liked nothing better than hearing praise from the nurses and doctors about her perfect figure and amazing acting talent. Those comments were music to her ears and better than the strongest tranquilizers. The recent events caused her anxiety to surface and she exhibited melodramatic behaviour. She was continuously calling her family doctor and the emergency psychiatric service, having suffered bouts of severe depression and anxiety since her infamous behaviour at the restaurant. On the other hand, her mischievous behaviour also brought her the attention that a diva craves. The minister of culture sent her a colourful bouquet of flowers wishing her a speedy recovery. Her fellow actors who had suffered less of her arrogance and abuse in her heyday, flocked in with flowers and chocolates.

On a sunny, cold, wintery morning, a nurse rushed in, her face radiant with excitement. 'Madame,' she cried.

'Mademoiselle, if you please,' Sandrine replied abruptly, interrupting the scared young nurse.

'Pardon. Madame Claudette phoned and she's asking to see you.'

Sandrine was sipping a cup of coffee that she'd poured accidentally on the white sheets, and covered them with dark stains. The nurse hurried to her rescue and cleaned up the mess.

'Claudette!' Sandrine's voice was loud and shaky. Her mind went back to the early sixties in her fame days when she was a winning horse at the French cinema and had been convinced to co-star with Claudette who was no less equal to her in fame and stardom. They shot the film in South America with full-blown scandals, having stolen one another's partners, fought on the set and had fierce competition over the film prizes. The hatred faded with the fade of their stardom. However, Claudette was more practical, less in denial and less problematic at work than Sandrine; she continued to pursue a career in acting much to Sandrine's envy. She wondered if Claudette was taking advantage of her fall to satisfy her long-awaited revenge. There was no way she was genuine and wanted to check on her. She felt like a dying lion waiting to be eaten by hyenas. *Was it defeat?* But no, not Sandrine who'd stood up to the studio moguls when female actresses were under the thumbs of cinema makers, producers and directors.

'*Pourquoi pas?*' she said with made-up confidence, pouring years of acting experience into her response. The terrified nurse was in fear of being on the frontline of offensive artillery between the two divas. She tried to hand the phone to Sandrine who asked the nurse to wait. She asked her to pass the mirror and gazed at her face, in an attempt to ignore her wrinkles, combed her hair to boost her confidence. She pointed in a theatrical gesture at the poor nurse to passed the phone and spoke in a reversed tone mimicking that of Marie Antoinette. '*Allo, oui.*'

'*Bonjour* Sandrine.'

'Ah, is that you Claudette?' Sandrine realised her tough facade could not hide her broken soul. Claudette reminded her of her success and failures. She continued to be the star even now. She had a family and children. Sandrine had nothing. Nevertheless, they had played the same part and were ready for a round like the good old days. Nothing had changed since the cat fights they had endured many moons ago. Now, it was all back in action and the camera was on.

Claudette picked up the thread. 'Sorry to hear you are not well. I learnt from the media about your breakdown,' she said. Her statement struck a chord, but Sandrine tried her best to control herself and follow the psychologist's instructions. 'It is stress darling, you know. Do you remember when you took an overdose when Robert left you?' Sandrine said in a defiant tone.

'Was that when you seduced him and persuaded him to leave me?' Claudette's tone was full of vengeance.

'Darling, it is a free market, demand and supply and the survival for the fittest,' Sandrine replied immediately.

'The fittest, not the bitchiest,' Claudette's response was prompt.

'Are you calling to satisfy your revenge?'

No, I am getting older and I wanted to settle old things in my life.'

'And am I part of your baggage?'

'Sandrine, it's all history. Why don't we put it behind us? I saw the humiliation you have endured recently. I felt sorry for you.'

Sandrine's blood was boiling. She could not stop herself from raising her voice.

'You know, it is no use. You are a bitch. I had to put up with you. You slept with producers and directors and stole a role made specially for me.'

'For you? A second-rate C lister.' Claudette's shouting deafened Sandrine.

'I won a César and acted in cinema and theatre,' Sandrine yelled. Her voice escalated and attracted the attention of the nurses and psychiatrists. They rushed in and Sandrine carried on with her shouting battle. They didn't dare take the phone away from her or cut off the call.

Claudette hung on, but Sandrine continued to swear at her. She threw the phone and hit the window opposite. The glass shattered and ruined the amazing view of the wooded scenery through the window. The hospital staff watched the scene that was like a lioness defending her cubs. 'I am Sandrine, don't you know? I was a starlet, a vedette, the diva of my day and I always will be.' The senior, grey-haired psychiatrist approached her. 'Mademoiselle Sandrine, you are the star. Please take this tablet.'

'You've seen my films doctor, haven't you?'

'I have not missed a single one.'

She changed her posture with a seductive gesture, showing that she still had it. She extended her hand to the doctor and took the tablet, and ignored the young nurse who handed her a glass of water.

She floated into sleep, dreaming of days gone by.

Chapter sixteen

The Eminent Union

Karim spent his days wandering Paris on foot in search of a job. He was ready to do anything to raise more money to achieve his goal. Doors were shut in his face. The French Government was making a desperate attempt to eliminate immigration from abroad and more so from the Middle East. The anti-immigration movement was fuelled by the far-right rhetoric that had been flourishing in the Western World. These movements claimed that economic immigrants would suck dry their livelihood.

In reality hard earnt cash was an exception for an immigrant in France. The benefits from social security were limited and hardly enough to keep food on the table. Karim walked miles and miles with no aim or result. He sat on a bench by the Seine River wondering if he had made the right choice by leaving his country and running after a mirage. But he had no choice but to flee the death and destruction for a peaceful life. He felt in his trousers where a bunch of banknotes was wrapped in a belt around his waist. He could not open a bank account or trust the authorities. He was concerned that they might confiscate his only precious possessions. In other words, the money. He took the opportunity to lock himself in a toilet to count the notes without his roommates being around and fear of it being stolen. The decision to try to get to the UK again after his shambolic near death experience was a difficult one. He stashed the money in a pocket under his belt. It was all he had apart from his dignity. His butchery work was under threat of being scrutinised by the police, and social services were trying to tighten the ring of illegal immigration; it was a critical time to bring his family from the refugee camps in Turkey to Europe.

He had saved four thousand euros. His money should serve the purpose; his dream of reaching the UK. But what about having a family reunion? It was a decision he had to make.

He dialled Souhaib on What's App.

'Alsalaam Alaykum.'

'Hello. I haven't seen you, not even in our shared accommodation.'

'Yes. I leave at four and return at ten p.m., and am working like a dog.'

'Yes. Life here is not as easy as our fellow countrymen think back home.'

'I know. I cannot stop sending money to family and friends,' Karim replied.

'Likewise.'

'Do you remember our discussions, Souhaib?'

'Of course, of course. Shall we catch up soon? Souhaib wanted to discontinue the dialogue abruptly, for fear of being overheard. He was convinced that foreigners were under the radar of the French intelligence censorship.

'Okay, I will wait for you at home.'

'No, I am staying with my girlfriend and we need some privacy to discuss such a sensitive issue.'

Karim got the coded message, having used it in his birthplace to evade Syrian estate censorship.

'Okay, where and when?' Karim asked.

'What about at seven p.m. at the Moroccan Café in Belleville.'

'I know it well, see you then.'

He hung up, full of hope for a new start. He felt the need to walk outdoors and went wandering in cold, dry Paris aimlessly. The early dark winter evening arrived early and woke him from his daydream to reality. He dashed up the steps speedily, eager to catch up with his friend. He got there fifteen minutes late and there was no sign of Souhaib. A young Algerian waiter approached him. *Alsalaam alaykum*. It has been a long time since I have seen you,' the waiter said.

'Busy with life. Normal black tea please.'

'Green or mint tea is the normal order here.' He laughed, teasing Karim who told him that mint tea smell reminded him when he was a sick child in Syria. His grandmother used to prepare it when he'd had a stomach ache.

The tea arrived on a cheap tin tray engraved with traditional geometric patterns and Quranic verses. Karim sipped the hot drink carefully to avoid scalding his tongue and then faster when it became cooler. Time went too slow with him downing a few cups until he ran out of patience and What's Apped Souhaib. He got no response. When he was about to leave when Souhaib dashed in out of breath.

'Sorry mate, I was very busy.'

'With your girlfriend?' Karim cooed in a naughty tone.

'And work too.'

'What are you doing?

'I am working in business. Import and export.' He changed the subject abruptly, giving a sign that he didn't want to go further with the discussion. He ushered Karim to sit in a quiet corner.

'I want to move on.'

'What do you mean?'

'I want to reunite with my family.'

'How?'

'I need them to join me.'

'I see. But they are in a refugee camp in Syria. Am I correct?'

'Yes. They are in camp on the Turkish border.'

'I thought so.'

'I want to bring them over.'

Souhaib gazed at his friend with a smirk. 'Do you realise how difficult that is?'

'I know, I have been there.'

'Of course, friend. You are single, but it is different with a family.'

'I understand. I can go and accompany them on the journey of hell,' Karim said as he re-lived his horrendous journey trans Europe — the claustrophobic feeling of being in a small space squeezed in with many other refugees in search of a better life. 'I want them to join me,' he added.

'How much money do you have?'

'Four thousands euros,' Karim said in a proud tone, having poured precious blood and sweat into his effort to raise the funds. His statement was received with a smirk by Souhaib who undermined his achievement. 'Is that all?'

'Yes. You can't imagine how much I suffered to collect that sum.'

'Of course. But you'll need more money to get a family of three here. You know what I mean.'

Karim looked puzzled and humiliated. He didn't know what to say.

Souhaib filled the silence. 'Listen. You have always dreamt of going to the UK.'

'Yes and I tried and failed.'

'The chances of having a family reunion are greater in the UK than in France. They do not want foreigners here.'

'Yes. I agree with you.'

'So the best option is for you to go there.'

The immediate flashbacks of the sinking dingy with the shouts of the drowning Asian girl penetrated his ears.

Chapter seventeen

Back to the Stage

The French media was busy with the news of up and coming stars and more so with politics from the British referendum and predictions of its aftermath and the economic difficulties France was encountering.

Sandrine was back on the shelf having entertained the older generation with her childish and immature behaviour, commencing with her infamous act at the restaurant followed by her admission to the mental health clinic, and ending with her unpleasant encounter with the other passé actress Claudette. Despite the adverse events Sandrine faced, she had enjoyed the limelight of the long gone good old days. She loved being the centre of attention with the world revolving around her. She never got fed up with her, *me, me* attitude.

Now, she was back to her lovely but boring life in her flat in Châtelet. The same routine of walking the dog or preparing coffee became a heavy chore and it was difficult to achieve without a helper. She hired a maid who worked a few hours a week provided Sandrine had no direct contact with her, and instructions were conveyed by the employment agency.

Sandrine protested, shouted, swore and kicked, but no one heard her.

'That is what you get,' she was told by the maid's employment agency manager.

It wasn't long before she put the nails in her coffin when she relentlessly cross-examined the new maid about her work and tried to undermine her.

'Enough is enough, I would rather to live off the social security than work for you,' said the maid.

Loneliness was what Sandrine became used to. Nevertheless, her recent unfortunate events reconnected her to the external world that she missed. She remembered a relatively recent interview with *Paris Match,* 'Have you chosen to be a recluse like Greta Garbo?' she was asked. She fixed her large black Chanel sunglasses, similar to the Hollywood legend, in place. 'Never. I am a very social person and like to be with others, contrary the general perception.'

Coming back from the recent past, she flicked through TV channels and magazines. They were boring. She grabbed her ancient yellow phone book which was full of crossed-out names and numbers of friends and acquaintances who had left her life because of arguments, fights, and disagreements and her famous comments. Her list of friends was dwindling by the day.

Sandrine had grown up in a middle-income household, but she educated herself when she left school at an early age and spent the daytime shooting films and evenings at the theatre. She rose above the others when she became the sex symbol of France.

While she was reflecting on her past, one name came to mind, Morris, who she befriended while shooting a film in northern France. He was a gay producer who had no sexual interest in her whatsoever. The lack of sexual interest made her appreciate herself for her brain rather than her flesh. She looked through her old, yellow phone book for names starting with M. She dialled the number.

'Morris, *ça va?*'

'Sandrine, what a pleasure to hear from you,' a soft manly voice said.

'Yes, but you never bothered to call after hearing what had happened to me.'

'Pardon, Sandrine. My partner Johnnie passed away.'

'Sorry.'

'C'est la vie. He suffered a great deal with cancer.'

'I am alone anyhow as always.' Her voice was bitter.

'Sandrine, You had many men who fell for you, but you turned all of them down.'

His preaching tone grated. 'They were all bad people.'

'But they couldn't be.'

'What, do you mean I am the problem?' she responded promptly in an angry tone.

'Maybe.'

'How dare you.' Her tone became menacing.

'Sandrine. I am honest and as a close friend I should tell you what I think. What has happened to your maid?' He tried to divert the subject to deescalate the situation.

'All gone.'

'Even the Arab boy?'

'Oh yes. He was very arrogant,' she said indifferently.

'Maybe proud.'

'I don't care.'

'Well, you should or you will start cleaning the house yourself.'

She could not continue the conversation and hung on one of her last loyal friends.

She turned the phone book pages and looked for the letter K. 'Useless!' she muttered in an angry tone.

Chapter eighteen

The Web of Deceit

Karim was waiting near the charming harbour of Saint-Malo in north-west France, facing the English Channel, where after contemplating the horizon, he imagined life with his family in England. Souhaib had arranged the escape plan to England, the promised paradise. He was told that he should wait for a person to collect him from a café close to the port, then he would travel by boat to England. He had been assured about security and guarantees, having paid the total sum of four thousands euros.

Earlier in the day, Karim had taken the train from Gare du Nord with minimal belongings having followed the smuggler's instructions. He carried several layers of clothing underneath his pants, extra socks and home-made sandwiches.

He sipped coffee in the café as he waited for a phone call that could change his life forever. The wait was long as he watched seagulls flying over Saint-Malo Harbour. The waiter had been bringing small cups of strong espresso which gave him reflux and burnt his throat. The wait was too long to stop his fidgety nervous gestures that attracted the unnecessary attention of the curious elderly locals. They found him a novelty in their tranquil retired lives.

He tried to call Souhaib without success. The phone was out of order. His mounting anxiety alerted the café's employers and clients alike. It was unusual to have tourists in cold winter, let alone Middle-Eastern looking ones. The town had been alerted by the numerous and most likely failed attempts of refugees trying to cross the English Channel in recent years. It had become a common topic of conversation.

He felt helpless as he tried to dial the numbers of the Syrian community in Paris and asked for Souhaib. Alarm bells began to ring that he had been conned by someone who said he was a friend.

His last resort was to call Haji; he was seeking comfort.

'Allo Haji, I am in trouble,' he started without a greeting.

'What has happened, son?'

'I am in Saint-Malo.'

'What are you doing there?'

'I paid a fellow countryman four thousands euros to take me to England and I have been waiting all day.' The silence from Haji mortified Karim. Was there worse to come?

'Oh no! You have been deceived. I've heard many horror stories such as this,' Haji said with some hesitation after a long thoughtful pause.

'Please no, I worked like a donkey for two years to raise that money.'

'You need to submit to God's will and consider it gone.'

'No. I must go, even if I swim to the other shore.' Karim was angry and anxious; aggressive and unbalanced in his thinking. He shouted and screamed in protest to the increasing suspicion of the café dwellers and owners alike.

A short time later, two French gendarmes stepped into the café and stood over him.

'Bonjour,' a young French policeman said in a firm tone.

'Bonjour,' Karim screamed.

'What is the problem?'

'Not your business,' Karim relied abruptly.

'Can you show us your papers?'

Karim refused to budge and pushed one of the policemen to the ground. The other one was quick to restrain and handcuff him. The café owner rushed to the policemen's rescue.

'Monsieur, I think he is from the jungle camp,' he said to the policeman.

The latter statement made the client's eyebrows raise in repulsion. The camp dwellers were indoctrinated by the far right movement about the Islamic invasion of France. There was not much public sympathy for refugees and Karim was no different. The policemen led him to the police car to take him to the local police station where his protests and objections would be ignored or responded to with shouting. The young policeman pushed him roughly into the police car. Karim's head hit the car's roof.

The journey to the police station was the longest ever. Karim had lost the plot after losing his money and losing his dream to reach the United Kingdom. He'd been conned twice, and lost a fortune after he had slaved day and night to achieve his dream of reaching the British shores with his family. The gendarme moved him by force into the station and then to a cell. Karim's screams seemed to reached the other side of the Channel with no response whatsoever.

What have I done? He had no answer to his conundrum and confusion. A young policeman with a goatee beard approached him. 'Monsieur, do you want a drink?' He extended a glass of water to Karim. Karim was very agitated and pushed the glass away, splashing water on the young policeman's uniform. His colleagues stood up like Samurai warriors to retaliate, but the young man ushered them to sit.

'Sorry sir, about what happened.' Karim scanned the cell and burst into tears as he asked the young policeman's forgiveness. Without thinking he rushed towards the policeman and hugged him. There was minimal resistance from the policeman but his boss was watching the scene with concern.

The young man handed Karim a tissue to wipe his flooding tears.

'Monsieur, in my country it's a shame for a man to cry,' Karim said out of the blue in fluent French.

'They say it is healthy to do so,' the young policeman replied.

Karim realised his gesture was inappropriate and pulled his heavy body away from the young man. 'Pardon. I was rude. I should not behave so.'

'No problem.' The young man smiled

After a while the young man brought him a baguette filled with cheese and tomato and reassured him that it had no bacon inside.

Karim has not eaten a bite since early in the morning. He munched the enormous sandwich quickly with just a few bites.

The senior officer approached Karim. 'Sorry, but you attacked a policeman in a public place and we have to charge you.'

'Sir, I am a law-abiding man. I was a teacher in my own country.'

'I can see that you are a professional and we would like to drop the charges, but we are obliged to take action in front of the public.'

'Please, I do not want to go to prison.'

The middle-aged policeman smiled and reminded him of his favourite late uncle in Syria. 'No, it's not that bad, but we require someone you know to bail you out.'

Karim thought about who could do that. He could not rely on his mates. Some were illegal refugees who had been denied asylum, and failed multiple attempts to escape. Then Haji came to mind. He asked the policeman if he would permit him use his phone to call a friend. After an hour of deliberations, the young policeman handed over his confiscated mobile after charging it. Karim searched anxiously for a rescue phone number. None of them were close or trusted. After all, how could he trust anybody.

The name Haji sprang to his fingers as he scrolled through his contacts. With some hesitation, he pressed the name. An answering machine asked him to leave his contact details. 'Allo Haji, this is Karim. I want to ask you a favour. I need to be bailed out. I am in prison. Please help me.' Karim had to hand the phone back to the officer.

He spent the night in the cell thinking of his saviour Haji and the shame he brought to his family with imprisonment. The night was one of the longest, apart from the one he spent in a truck from Hungry to Paris. He woke in the morning to the voice of the morning-shift policemen. A pretty, petit white French policewoman approached him with coffee.'

'Bonjour.'

'Bonjour,' he replied as he took the strong coffee and downed it immediately. 'Can I have my phone please?' She took a minute to appraise his request with some reflection. She was not expecting his request and explained to her boss the whole story of the unfortunate Syrian man. She came back with his mobile. He pressed the button to listen to the voicemail to hear a message. It was from Haji. His heart was pounding. He wanted to get out from the cell. The message played in a sad voice, not the cheerful and positive person he knew. He was in shock and re-played the message a few times. *Sorry, Karim. I cannot help you. I have some problems with the police and my wife threatened to leave me if I bail you out. She thinks you are a baddie from the old days.* His hand relaxed and he dropped the mobile on the floor. The policewoman picked it up and tried to hand it back to Karim. He showed no interest. 'Monsieur. You need to call a friend or family to get you out.'

'I have none.'

'Quel dommage!'

As she was walking away with the phone Karim cried out. 'Mademoiselle, stop.'

She turned with fear on her face. 'I want to make a phone call.' He took the phone and scrolled to a number and pressed.

A tired voice answered. *'Allo, oui?'*

'Mademoiselle Sandrine,' Karim replied with a husky voice.

'Oui?'

'It is Karim.'

Chapter nineteen

The Summit

The Parisian winter had become harsh and longer than the norm. But the resilient Parisians never gave up their lifestyle, etiquette and elegance, neither harsh weather nor two world wars could bring that glamorous city to its knees.

Châtelet was no different. The posh district dwellers showed their designer clothes and jewels at every possible occasion and place.

Karim was walking alongside the Seine passing Pont Neuf, facing the harsh cold wind which was kinder than the bitter reality. He'd had to bow to life like a tree bending in the storm.

Sandrine's sarcastic remarks and her facial dissatisfaction at the slightest lack of accuracy and precision in following her unrealistic instructions echoed in his ears and played in front of his eyes. He had agreed to manage her flat fulfilling the job of a full-time maid. He recalled the phone call with Sandrine when they had both reached a critical point of desperate need for each other. Karim felt at rock-bottom after losing his money, his dreams and his pride after being rejected by everyone but her. He had spoken to a gendarme who was a big admirer of hers and he agreed to drop the assault charges against the policeman and Karim was released.

It was out of character for Sandrine to do so, but deep down she was feeling humiliated that no maid wanted to work for her. Karim's phone call was the glimmer of hope that she needed. She remembered that *arrogant Arab* as she used to call him. His voice was strong, echoing the desert depth and his olive skin matched his beard. She thought of their age difference, thirty-something junior to her, if not more. No way for a match, and she would never be associated with an Arab, a Muslim, let alone a refugee, it was a disaster and against all her principles.

Karim had to put up with her changeable, volatile moods. One minute she was soft, sweet and even flirty then for no reason she switched to being rude, horrible, shouting and exhibiting anger by throwing things and even swearing. He had to adapt to his new life. He had been through worse.

Moreover, the French authorities had barred him from having access to social security benefits, which were scarce any way, hardly enough to feed him or pay the rent, let alone support his family. There was no chance in heaven to get a job with cash in hand at the butcher's market or anywhere else. Security had been tightened.

At times, he had to calm her down, but she apologised afterwards on rare occasions.

The reunion was hard for both of them. Each wanted to show that the other had more need and not vice versa.

Karim was wiping the marble table crowded with Sandrine's photos from films and real life shots. While he was dusted the framed photos, a medium-sized photo of a young blonde and very beautiful girl caught his attention. 'Wow!' he said in a quiet voice.

From nowhere, he heard a voice in French. '*Elle est très belle.*'

'Yes, of course. She is beautiful,' Karim replied avoiding eye contact with the diva slowly walking towards him.

'I was eighteen and had just started acting. I was pure and innocent,' she cooed with a sigh.

'But very beautiful.' He raised his eyes to meet hers.

She turned to the large Venetian mirror occupying the centre of the living room.

'Oh no, look at my wrinkles. I am old, not good-looking, nobody wants me,' Sandrine shouted. She threw a small Indian ivory box at the mirror and started crying and collapsing, but she was rescued by Karim and she found herself in his arms. When was the last time she'd been held by a man? Sandrine could not remember. She had missed a man's hold and the warmth of breath she needed. She raised her head and reached for his thick, dishevelled beard and planted a faint kiss on his rough lips that oozed masculinity. Karim succumbed to the emotions and to his physical needs. He'd been deprived of sex because he was loyal to his wife and religious affiliations. He felt urges taking over, but images of his wife and children stood in between. He pushed her gently aside with embarrassment at his hardening.

'Sorry, I cannot do it,' he said in an apologetic tone.

Sandrine could not cope with rejection or sheer humiliation. 'Who do you think you are? The likes of you can only dream of having a glimpse of Sandrine La Croix. You are nothing.' She raised her hand to slap Karim, but he evaded her with his youthful steps and rushed to the main door. 'You are mad. I feel sorry for you,' he said as he turned briefly.

She heard the door shut violently. Sandrine could not bear her weak body and she lay on the marble floor covered with Persian Kashan carpet. She was weeping. *Why am I doing this to myself?* She crawled along the cold marble floor to reach the phone.

Chapter twenty

Glamour to Belleville

Spring arrived and Paris changed. The clear, brighter blue skies of spring illuminated the La Cité de la Lumière. Sunny spells lifted the Parisian's sprits and their moods. Bellville held a monthly market that attracted all those from different walks of life. Those with low income could hardly afford the basic shopping and few could afford the luxuries and grabbed only the bargains.

In a building close by, Karim sat on the floor in a room he shared with two fellow countrymen. There were endless disputes about cleaning the room and the communal toilets. Each dweller wished that his roommate would not take long in the toilet or argue about the availability of hot water. It seemed too much for him to cope with all that stress. With the failure to reach England for the second time in a row, and then the insult from Sandrine; it was too much. He could not cope with her arrogance and rudeness undermining his capability and exhausting his patience to be respectful to an older woman. He burst into tears while having a fight with his housemates for no apparent reason.

Needless to say, weakness was not his forte. He had a shortage of cash, having lost all his savings to the crooks who were scavenging millions and millions from others' misery. And he had lost his right to social security benefits in France. Since Sandrine sacked him or he left her, depending on the way each thought about it, he had no spare cash to support his family, let alone to feed himself. He left the room in the midst of the shouting of his roommates and ignored them.

He wandered in the Belleville market and examined faces and people's reactions without pettiness from others. His pride came first. While he was walking aimlessly, a voice called to him, 'Karim! Karim!'

He turned with fear. Was it someone wanting to remind him of his failures or to offer patronising advice?

But he received a sweet smile from Haji. He walked towards him maintaining minimal eye contact.

'*Alsalaam alaykum,*' Karim's said in the tone of a defeated man.

'Come on, son. Why didn't you come to me?' Haji patted his back.

'To tell you what? Of my failure?'

'Why do you say that? It is always determination and persistence that are the rules of the life game.'

'I am useless.' Karim burst into tears.

'Never give up. I am sorry if I have betrayed you. It was difficult having undergone life's pressures. My wife was about to leave me with three children.'

Haji's words revived his hopes and dreams that were mixed with shame about his behaviour. 'Not to worry. Nobody is perfect. I understand your position.' Karim seemed to have forgiven him.

'Listen, you have to prepare yourself for another round.' Haji's reassurance in a confident tone intimidated Karim about the unknown which was yet to come.

'No, no, I couldn't.' Karim was trembling.

'You should. It is *repot du gurerrier* according to the French saying.'

Karim laughed. 'The warrior's rest. Warriors never rest, after all. They start fighting after the rest.'

'Listen, I have a friend who sells flowers and plants on his stall, it's not far away and he needs someone to help him. Your French has improved significantly.' Haji's dialogue took a different turn.

'Can I handle it? I doubt that I could.'

'You will. You have to. The secret of the game of survival is perseverance.' Haji dialled a number learnt by heart with his old mobile and started chatting in French indispersed with Arabic with religious meaning.

'He is waiting for you. Haji handed him the directions to where the stall was situated a few yards away.

Karim started his new job the same day and he handled the stall so well that his boss, a second generation Moroccan man, running his flower business all over Paris, trusted him and left him by himself. Karim adapted to the new job in a haste that meant he could pay his rent and it also enabled him to buy simple meals and make the occasional phone call to his family.

He did not have the heart to tell Fadwa of his latest failed adventure, which would break her heart and her hopes.

The days went by with the same monotonous rhythm only interrupted by a difficult abusive client or a fight over the toilet or a bitter conversation with his wife about her miserable life in the refugee camp in Turkey.

One day on a relatively sunny but chilly day while Karim was arranging the flowers, a short, slim woman wearing a yellow Chanel suit covered with a faux-fur coat, and wearing a matching large yellow hat that covered her face which was disproportionate to her petit body, appeared. She was walking her barking poodle that was taking the lead.

'*Bonjour,*' a soft feminine voice cooed as if it was coming from a different world or the radio next to him. Karim was not used to such clients; not in the Belleville market. He tried to look at the source of the voice, but the sharp, bright, golden rays of the Parisian spring sun blinded him. Many thoughts crept into his mind. Who was she? The older generation may well have guessed that she was *Sandrine la belle* as she was called in her heyday. Some of the customers stopped what they were doing and glanced with curiosity at the woman who had come from the other world.

'*Bonjour.* How can I help you, mam?' Karim asked politely.

'I am sure you can.' She raised her face, lifted the edge of the hat, and showed her face that had an ancient beauty. The Parisian make-up could not hide the lines made by years of interesting events. Karim was taken by surprise. Sandrine, what are you doing here?' he shouted.

'I am a client or it is illegal to buy flowers?' Her theatrical tone softened his strong reaction.

'No, I did not mean ... how can I help you?' He was fearful of losing his job.

'I need a home helper.'

'Madame, this a flower stall,' he replied in a professional manner.

'I want to see the owner of the stall.' Sandrine uttered her words with a hint of seduction.

'You can advertise asking for helpers.' Karim felt he had the upper hand.

'I have, but I could not find a suitable one. It is difficult to find someone nowadays.' Her arrogance prevented her from admitting the reality that everybody knew.

'Why me?' Karim asked.

'You are different.' She paused and looked at his hazel eyes with curiosity and lust while he avoided eye contact with her.

Her flattering words did wonders, like music to his ears. He needed something positive.

'I think you did an excellent job. I miss your humour,' she added.

'Mam, it is difficult to work for you. I could not cope with the insults and humiliation. Yes, I am poor but equally proud.'

'I am sorry if I insulted you. Please forgive me. I will pay you much more. Please come back.'

Karim looked at her eyes. *Could people change so fast*? He was in desperate need of cash to support his family. More so, his life costs in Paris and maybe his dream to reach the UK. *Oh no not again. It must be a curse.* The voice became louder and in Arabic. He glanced at Sandrine's blue eyes, she had been pretty once upon a time. He remembered Googling photos of her in her youth. She was hot. Actually, she still had it. He was working like a dog under extreme weather conditions from the hot sun to the chilly wind to earn a few euros a day.

'You are an intelligent and skilled man. You do not want to spend your life behind this stall working day and night and earning nothing. I will pay you more.' She struck while the iron was hot.

Karim turned to check over his shoulder. *'D'accord.'*

She smiled cunningly after winning the first round. *At last, I have a man under my thumb as I always had.*

I will tame the tigress.

They exchanged smiles after signing an unwritten truce. But for how long?

Chapter twenty-one

Life like Others

The spring came with a vengeance, making Paris brighter. The Hôtel de Ville was shining with golden rays; reflections that blinded Karim's unprotected eyes.

He was making the journey from Belleville to Châtelet on foot and by bus, avoiding the centre of Paris to save some money. He was counting every cent to save for his family at the refugee camp.

Unsurprisingly, working with Sandrine had been a bumpy ride that he is trying to cope with. She could not stop giving orders or being patronising. He often ran out of patience and had to practise self-restraint. Too hard heads met tête-à-tête. If Karim said it was white, she objected, it was black. He reached the building feeling energetic, and opened the back door allocated for the servants and made his way to the flat. Fierce negotiations shrouded with mistrust and suspicion from Sandrine were the normal start to the day.

His daily routine entailed taking charge of the cleaning, and general maintenance of the old eighteenth-century apartment. The most difficult task was being in charge of the shopping that never pleased Sandrine.

He arrived early in the morning like an intruder, trying not to make noise to upset the dog that would engage in a barking session to alert his mistress.

Sandrine's continued to suffer an interrupted sleep pattern or lack of sleep. It was her ongoing complaint. She drank a few glasses of Champagne in the hope that it would provide her with a decent sleep; it wasn't fruitful. Her insomnia, alcohol and mood dysfunction were a perpetuating prophecy.

Karim heard shouting. 'Who is that?' It was resonating with the barking dog. 'It is Karim,' he replied.

'Do not shout; I am not deaf,' she replied in an aggressive tone.

He swallowed her comment and started clearing the kitchen table where there were pieces of cheese and a rotten tomato that could attract mice. The champagne flutes were stained with lipstick prints reflecting well-defined lips. Since having been a practising Muslim after the war, he refrained from drinking alcohol. *May God forgive me.* He washed the dishes and cleaned the table. All of sudden an authoritarian voice erupted like a volcano. 'Pardon, I want coffee.' Her voice pierced his ears. He sighed heavily. 'God give me patience.' As usual Sandrine was recovering from a hangover.

They had an agreement that he would not prepare food or be asked to serve beverages, particularly alcohol. Well coffee was something he could do. He looked for the coffee machine and was unable to locate the coffee plunger. He was used to having Turkish coffee and instant coffee. Nevertheless, he learnt that instant coffee was low life in France and in the West generally and he would have make a fresh brew. He rushed to hide his cheap coffee jar in the kitchen cupboard. He was in a hurry to add the boiling water to the freshly ground coffee in the cafetière. A delicious smell filled the air. He realised Sandrine's calorie count would be his pain. She continued to dwell on her high calorific intake, blaming Karim for an extra carrot or tomatoes in her lunch or an extra drop of olive oil in her favourite humus. Her main meal consisted of only salad. He once dared to confront her about her low dietary intake, but she answered abruptly. 'It is personal.'

'I am just worried about your health.' His reply came a surprise to her.

'It is not your business,' she answered back but with joy, knowing someone cared about her.

Karim prepared his usual lunch at home or at Sandrine's. He munched humus with fresh pitta bread and tabouli. He dug in with his hands dipping them into the humus dip and ate big pieces of bread soaked with olive oil.

Once, Sandrine entered the kitchen and showed surprise at him eating with his hands. And he was so embarrassed he tried to hide his hands that were stained with humus and olive oil; he swallowed a big chunk of bread that almost choked him. She rushed to him with a glass of water and hit his back with a disproportionate force in relation to her tiny feeble body, then she squeezed his body to her chest. 'Take it easy,' she shouted in panic.

His face blushed, then turned blue. Karim was trying to cough, gasping for air. Sandrine shouted *au secours* but got no response. The dog was barking madly. She came closer to Karim and held him as she tried to tap the back of his chest, then she tried the Heimlich manoeuvre, but her strength was no match for his strong body. After several attempts at pushing his diaphragm with her hands, Karim regained his proper breathing and muttered an apology. 'Sorry, I was hungry.' Sandrine had forgotten the meaning of the word hunger after years and years of dieting and restriction of her food intake. 'I suppose people do get hungry. You should not be ashamed,' she replied in a faint voice. Karim's eyes met her pure dark-blue ones, sensing the human side of her. 'Thank you, you saved my life.'

'Did I?' she said with a smile full of pride.

He offered her the Middle-Eastern traditional food. She declined. *'Non merci.* Are you still hungry?' They laughed loudly.

She walked to the door at a pace of a young woman then turned to Karim. 'By the way, do you know that there are forks and spoons in the drawer. That is how we eat with in France.' He looked at the angle of her eyes and her superior attitude as she left the kitchen triumphantly.

You cannot teach an old dog a new trick.

Chapter twenty-two

Come and Dine with Me

Sandrine had hardly left her flat since her scandal at the restaurant, apart from popping to the shop or walking the dog in the park in a disguise with dark sunglasses and large hat hiding her fine features. She relied on Karim to do her shopping but resented having fights with him when he refused to buy her alcohol. He declined the task at first but eventually succumbed to her wishes. Nevertheless, they agreed to disagree by having a truce that Sandrine would manage the alcohol and the dog and Karim would handle the rest of her affairs.

Bit by bit, she started to leave home with Karim's support. Sandrine often wore a pink Chanel dress, colour coordinated with Pierre Hardy shoes. She recalled the days when the designers fought for her approval for her to advertise their dresses and accessories but not anymore and now she had to foot the bill. Karim followed her and the dog in a parade where she wanted to show the *public princess surrounded by her entourage.* But Karim was anxious about walking with her in the park and tried to distance himself from her to save himself the embarrassment of being humiliated, after one of her expected or unexpected outbursts. She sat on a bench after setting free her dog, who began playing with other dogs and ignoring his controlling master's orders. Sandrine wished to be seen accompanied by a young, handsome man; she had a tendency to show off in front of the Parisian aristocratic ladies with her toyboy, but equally she did not want to associate with his modest background, particularly with him being Middle Eastern and a Muslim. But beggars couldn't be choosers. He was all what she could get.

Sandrine scrutinised Karim by lowering her sunglasses. A strong build, with muscular arms from his manual work. She remembered how strong he was when he carried her to bed, after she had passed out after a heavy alcohol binge. She woke from her daydream to the sound of her barking dog while Karim was trying to avoid attending him. 'He does not bite,' she hissed in his ear.

'I am not afraid of a dog,' he responded in a humiliated macho tone.

'Really!' She uttered her words with a loud laugh, distracting the dog walkers from their dogs and much to Karim's embarrassment.

He bit his lip out of anger. 'I will go and get coffee,' he muttered.

'Espresso with no sugar, please.' Her confident, certain tone came surprised him.

Damn life when it turns against you. Why should I put up with her arrogance and belittling behaviour? Then he thought of his wife and children in derelict conditions at camp. And he knew that he would never forget England.

Days went by and they got used to the company of each other, passing time together or just passing like ships in the night, trying to minimise contact but equally wanting to shout at each other. Sandrine threw tantrums, and avoided pouring her anger and frustration directly on Karim. He wanted to appease her. Days continued to pass. And they learnt to co-habit trying to get used to each other because they needed each other.

On a warm, late spring evening, Karim had finished the cleaning and shopping in the early evening. He popped into living room where Sandrine had uncorked her Champagne Louis Roederer Cristal. She was sipping it and lying on her gilded lounger that she prided herself in using when she had played the French Queen Marie de Médici at the end of her acting career. She had never got out of that acting role. Her light, white-chiffon dress revealed her tiny shrinking breasts with some evidence of long-gone beauty from her prime. She turned her body in a seductive manner that moved something in Karim who had not come so close to a woman since leaving his wife in his native country. He remembered as a teenager the culture of sex segregation; anything would stimulate him even Sandrine. She ushered him with a gentle tone. 'Please sit down.'

Karim was in shock following the 360 degree change in her behaviour. He could not answer her in English, French or even Arabic, and he found it difficult to swallow with a dry mouth and mounting anxiety.

'Thanks, mam, I have to go home,' he uttered his words with difficulty as he took in her lust.

His decline was humiliating to a vedette who all men begged to have a glimpse of, once upon the time. 'Are you going to sit in your lovely room alone?' Her tone was full with sarcasm borne of humiliation.

'The place is decent with good people, mam,' he replied with pride.

Sandrine felt the impact of her sarcastic remark if not psychopathic comment that hurt his feelings. She sat upright in a semi-official position, wanting to mend the damage but not knowing how. It was the first time she had regretted saying something despite having an insight into the reason of having non-lasting relationships personally and professionally. 'I thought you were lonely. That's all,' she added.

'And you?' he responded in a warm tone.

'Very much so. Please hang around.' Her begging tone pierced his ears with surprise.

'Please sit down. What do you like to drink? This is not the best Champagne on earth but it is high quality.'

'Sorry, I do not drink.'

'Strange, never had a drink?'

'I used to drink. It was more acceptable to drink alcohol when I was very young. My father used to drink arak or beer but never Champagne. I had to prepare meza with the arak.'

'Arak?' she asked with a curious tone.

'Arak is like Greek ozo.'

'In France, we have pastis with anise flavour.' She came closer to Karim. 'Would you cheat and have a drink?'

He contemplated the coffee table lined with a plate of olives, crisps and a bowl of plain salad that was her only meal of the day.

'Come on, go and get yourself a glass.' She extended her hand, pointing at the alcohol bottle.

He stood upright and walked towards the kitchen. 'Make sure it is a Champagne flute and crystal,' Sandrine shouted. 'Ah and do not forget to bring the humus too.' She raised her voice.

Karim smirked; how hungry she was. He came back with the glass and the humus tub with pitta bread.

'I made it myself,' he said as he placed the humus plate in front of her with immense pride.

Sandrine poured the Champagne into his glass. 'Salut,' she said.

'Cheers,' he reciprocated.

Their glasses clinked and the same with their eyes. There was a lot of desire.

'Pass me the humus please.' She submitted to her body's needs.

Karim stood up to save his embarrassment for not bringing the cutlery.

'I will get you a spoon.'

'No need.' I will use my hands.' She held his hands with affection.

Karim sipped from his glass and sipped again followed by another until they became closer and closer. Sandrine approached his lips.

'I may need to go home; it is late,' he said.

'Never too late.' She held his head and pushed her soft lips with their Christian Louboutin lipstick to his strong jaws. Her lips touched his. And the rest is history.

Chapter twenty-three

Another Day, a Different Day

Early Sunday morning the sound of bells from the next door church pierced Sandrine's ears. They would not help her ongoing morning headache caused by a hangover that reflected her problem with drinking. She felt as if her brain was about to explode. She was used to late nights shrouded by alcohol and even illicit drugs in her youth. She realised that her old, tiny body could no longer cope with that amount of alcohol. Equally, she was not a spring chicken anymore; yet she was in constant denial of this.

A trail of memories passed as she remembered her previous alcohol-related incidents: blackouts where she found herself in different hotels with different men and even found herself in the bed of another female star known for her bi-sexual liaisons. That could have a crushed her career back then. Since then she had been trying to limit her alcohol intake with no success. It compensated for her poor diet to maintain her slim figure — an unlimited obsession. She searched her body to feel if she was unclothed. The last trace of her memory was with Karim in the living room and now she was in her bedroom. All of a sudden she heard snoring that became stronger and to her surprise she turned to see the naked body of a young man. She was familiar with his olive-skinned face with its well-defined beard. She was mortified and swore in her native tongue. How could it happen? She had always fancied younger men and Karim was no exception. She examined his muscular body and her memories took her to the night when they were drunk and they had started kissing and he had carried her to her bedroom. And the rest is vague history.

'*Merde,*' she shouted. Karim was in a deep sleep, like a semi-coma; the alcohol had played with his head. She shook his strong body with difficulty. 'Wake up!' He opened his eyes and saw Sandrine covering her wrinkled thighs with a bed sheet. 'What are you doing in my bed?' she asked. He was taken by surprise that her fifty-something years of experience at lovemaking had got him into her bed. He tried to explain to her what had happened the night before, but he was talking to his hands in the face of her shouting and accusing him of raping her. He tried to calm her down, knowing the fragility of his position and how he could not defend himself — poor Muslim immigrant versus a French national symbol in an electrified atmosphere where the far right was producing noise about the mass immigration from the East. Karim burst into tears whispering for forgiveness from God, thinking that he was being punished for drinking alcohol and committing adultery. On a similar note, Sandrine was exhibiting her frenzy and hysteria with a loud blubbering. After some turbulence, she chose to come to her senses, remembering slowly and surely the events of last night when she and Karim had become intoxicated. It did not take Karim many glasses to approach Sandrine and caress her until she felt numb. He remembered that after downing a few glasses of Champagne, she had started hugging him warmly and kissing him all over. She had jumped over him like a hungry tigress chasing her prey to feed her hungry cubs. They ended up in her bedroom on her bed.

They sat in peace on the bed back to back. He was terrified about what would happen, fearful of God, but even so, he had enjoyed the pleasures of the flesh after a very long time of deprivation.

Although she blamed herself for her stupidity, she realised how much she had missed the warm hold of a man. Karim was a tiger, having not been intimate for a long time. The atmosphere became calmer as they turned their trunks slowly and faced each other. They uttered the same words at the same time. 'Are you okay?'

Chapter twenty-four

Let's Sing

As the days went by, Karim and Sandrine kept the truce alive and have tried to be civil to each other but were equally guarded. He tried hopelessly to approach her. Her reception was variable from welcoming to avoidant to being clingy depending on her mood, which he gauged carefully like the Parisian weather forecast.

They carried on their daily routine: she was drinking, walking the dog and occasionally shopping while Karim did the house chores besides preparing his Middle-Eastern recipes despite Sandrine complaining that she was putting on weight despite her significant decline in drinking alcohol. Nevertheless, she continued to blame Karim, the Middle East and everyone but herself. Karim got used to her shouts of horror when she attempted to weigh herself on the scales in the bathroom.

One evening, while Karim was doing the washing after serving Sandrine dinner, he realised how tired he felt after preparing a Syrian meal that could be a poor man's meal. It consisted of pitta bread stuffed with feta cheese, humus and labneh. Sandrine declined dining with him but was curious to watch as Karim devoured big portions of toasted pitta bread immersed with humus and dripping with olive oil. She approached him slowly like a mouse waiting for cheese, and sat next to him. He pushed the plates towards her with hesitation. He brought the food closer and closer to her until she started eating.

'Do you want me to bring your alcoholic drink?' he whispered in fear of an unexpected response.

'*Non Merci*, I will drink strong tea with you.' Her voice was breaking.

More days went by; the two of them could not live with or without each other.

He could not find another lucrative job to save money to bring his family to France. The French studios boycotted Sandrine and agencies renounced her for rudeness and deemed it impossible to work with her. Karim learnt where and when to approach her.

Once in while he had a breakdown over a strong cup of black, sweet tea. He started browsing on his mobile phone searching desperately for news about Syria. His eyes followed the endless links with ever-depressing news of killing and bloodshed. His attention diverted to the Arabic entertainment section on the websites to escape the bitter reality. He went to YouTube to look for old Arabic songs. His mother had fallen in love with the Egyptian Singer Abdul Halim Hafez and his equally famous female co-star Shadia singing the love song on a late sixties hit film *Maabodat El Gamahir*, which means the beloved diva. It is the Pygmalion saga of a famous diva star and the poor actor, stealing a few minutes together cycling and singing as they travelled along the Nile River, escaping the pressure of her life of fame and attention and riding a bike touring the streets of Cairo. The film and the songs were the perfect distraction to the angry masses in Arab countries after the 1967 Arab-Israeli defeat.

Karim drifted away with the scene that reminded him of his mother who used to sing it when he was young. She could have been in despair over her long-gone love after being forced to marry her cousin (Karim's father) and not the neighbour she loved.

Noise came from the living room to the kitchen with an increasing intensity and hurried steps. Sandrine barged in shouting and holding her glass of white wine. 'Can't you hear. I am calling you. What is that noise you are making?' She pointed with her well-manicured nails.

Karim woke up from a lovely dream to a real-life nightmare 'May God give me the strength,' he murmured in Arabic. His reaction infuriated her that she increased the volume of her voice. 'What are you saying? You are not swearing in whatever tongue you are speaking in, are you?' She threw the wine glass.

Karim patiently picked it up. 'It is Arabic language and proper language. It was well established before your French.'

'Hah!' She turned with theatrical arrogance, looked daggers at him and dashed to the fridge.

'Can I help you?' Karim asked.

'I know my fridge well.' She looked inside it and searched, then turned to Karim. 'Where is the humus?'

'I thought you did not like it.'

'Actually, I was reading about it. It seems healthy and reasonably low in calories.'

'Is that what matters,' he said quietly.

'Où est-ce?'

'No, it's in the back. I've bought one from the supermarket. The big tub is home-made.'

She turned with a glance and inspected the fridge contents that she had deprived herself of for many years.

'Suit yourself.' He turned his back on her in an attempt to hide his anger. She grabbed the humus pot and a few peeled and chopped carrots to dip into it before she picked up her empty glass.

'Luckily, it's not cracked. You see, I bought it in Prague while we were shooting a film at the time of communist rule.' She danced around in the kitchen waltzing until she came closer to Karim with struggling weak knees that could hardly hold her upright. She turned to him. 'Does your wife do belly dancing?'

He felt uncomfortable, unwilling to discuss private matters; he tried to ignore her remark. She changed the subject. 'Why don't you come and sit with me in the living room.'

'Well. I have to go.'

'Where?'

'Home.'

'Your room.' Her tone was derogatory, full of disgust.

'Still, it is my home.'

'I feel lonely and I am bored and you are too. Why don't we keep each other company?'

'Mam, I am a poor man and I do not want to be on the wrong side of the law.'

'You mean I am unpredictable. Sorry about the other day. It was a surprise. I haven't been in such a situation for a long time. I had almost forgotten intimate times.'

'I'm sorry, but you made advances and I could not resist …'

'What!' she said with joy, waiting to hear how he had been mesmerised by her beauty and her gorgeous body.

'I am a man and excuse me; I was horny. I could not do anything to stop it.' He gazed at the floor out of shame.

Sandrine had a semi-fit and she turned with a panicky face as if she had met a ghost. 'I know men are pigs. They get what they want and leave. You used me.'

'Please do not get me wrong. I did not want to use you for sex. There is passion,' he said in a quiet voice.

His words were soothing to her battered ego.

'Can you transfer the Egyptian song to TV? I think there is a YouTube channel in my TV package. I don't know how to work it.' She took the expensive bottle of Champagne from the fridge with two flutes and walked towards the kitchen door, then she stopped and turned. 'Ah, please do not forget to bring the humus.' She walked with unstable steps shaking her tiny body and muttering the Arabic lovers' song, mastering the tone but not the words. Karim joined in. *'Alashan Ehna ma badena, wil awal mara le wahdenah'*. We are together for the first time.

Chapter twenty-five

Life is Full of Surprises

Paris was trying to get over a cold winter. It was the end of February and spring was at the door. The Parisians changed their coats to lighter and more colourful ones; both men and women paraded, showing off their new clothes with brighter colours in keeping with Parisian elegance and glamour.

Chatelet was no different and the high-heeled Parisians showed more than clothes but jewellery and watches, glittering under the golden rays of the sun which they had waited for impatiently.

Sandrine mingled with the crowds in the local park, led by her dog, unable to keep up with his fast steps. She curled her lip in disdain at the young and even more at the middle-aged women who dared to put on jeans topped by scruffy pullovers and a raincoat on such a sunny day. *Dégulus*. Low lives.' Her smartphone rang and she tried to find it in her Louis Vuitton handbag. She searched, trying to feel the vibration, but all she could feel was her Chanel number 5 perfume bottle. Her loyal brand since her early twenties. She pressed all the buttons and to her embarrassment bystanders showered her with curious looks and reminded her of her old age. She had purchased the smartphone at Karim's insistence and persistence that she should have one for emergencies. He also persuaded her to open Facebook and Twitter accounts to secure future work. Finally, she managed to operate the phone. Her voice was hostile. '*Oui?*'

'It's me, Sandrine.'

Karim's voice appeared to calm her down with immediate effect. 'Are you okay?'

'Yes thanks, why are you late?' she hissed with a turbulent voice.

I have had to collect a letter sent by special courier.' Karim's tone was obedient. 'And so ...'

'It must be important.'

'Can you identify the sender?' she asked.

'My reading and writing French is not up to standard.'

'Okay, bring it along.'

'Where are you?'

'Do I have to tell you every time? I am next to the fountain. You must know.' Her dismissive tone came to the attention of the park dwellers.

'May God give me strength,' Karim murmured in Arabic.

'What did you say?'

'No, nothing. I am on my way.'

Sandrine was engulfed with degradation and shame. It was not her generation, not her game. She tried hard to weather the IT revolution: buying a computer, having an IT teacher and allocated learning time with no success whatsoever. The same was true of social media until Karim had convinced her to get involved in the social media game. She became totally reliant on him after he mastered the basics of the French language.

She was impatient and jittery, anxious about the special delivery, and a trail of melancholic thoughts of death started to creep up on her ranging from her terminally ill mother's death to her alienated sister's death.

The dog was licking her legs, asking her to walk him, she declined his request and pulled her legs away, leaving the poor beast disappointed.

Karim appeared over the horizon. He looked slimer and taller than she perceived him.

'What a handsome young man he is,' she murmured in a quiet voice. His appearance perked up her mood and scattered the melancholic thoughts invading her mind. Karim approached her. 'Where have you been?' she screamed.

'I came immediately after I called you.'

'Excuses, excuses. I cannot trust anyone. Where is the letter?'

Karim produced a yellow envelope with gold edges and handed it over to her.

'What?' She extended her shaking hand and withdrew it immediately. 'No I cannot.' Her face was a mix of surprise and panic.

Karim was shocked by her unexpected reaction. He held the letter, not knowing what to do with it and sat down next to her. 'Are you okay?' he asked softly.

She hugged him warmly and sobbed. 'I cannot open letters. It will be bad news. By letter I have received news of the deaths of my parents, the love of my life's departure and the loss of major roles in films.'

His comfort reassured her; he held her hands with his strong, rough hand that reminded her of her femininity.

'I have a similar fear each time my mobile makes a noise; I think one of my family is dead. I know what you mean.'

'Sorry, you must have went through a lot, dear. I cannot imagine how you survived your boat trip to England. Thanks for trusting me.' She looked at him with her eyelids half closed.

'I feel better when I tell you,' he added.

'Please talk to me,' she uttered her words in a begging tone; not her usual self.

'Yes, only when you are in a good mood.' His tone was hesitant for fear of a sudden outburst from her.

She pulled her tiny body away from Karim and stood upright. 'Do you mean I am a volatile person?' Her tone changed; it was as if another person was talking to him.

The poor soul was mortified about her unexpected reaction had stemmed from paranoia. 'I didn't mean to …'

The dog barking at Karim drew her attention to the fact that she was being watched by the crowd. Out of shame she pulled her mink coat collar up to hide some of her face. She could have been recognised by the older generation in the park. Just then an old man rushed to her rescue, thinking the young man was harassing her. Sandrine thanked him. 'He is my assistant,' she said in a superior tone.

She turned to Karim who felt humiliated. 'Please, you open it for me.'

'Do you want to wait until we go home?' He was wary of her unexpected reaction.

'No, I must face the music. Now or never.' Her confident tone surprised him as did her ever- changing mood.

Karim opened the envelope with trembling hands. He could barely read French, let alone sophisticated high-level French. He looked at her. 'Go on read it aloud,' she said.

He started to read slowly with a heavy Middle-Eastern accent that was hard to comprehend.

'Cher Mademoiselle La Croix.'

'Come on spell it out. Who is the sender?' She gave him instructions in a rude tone.

'The … I am not sure it is a strange name.'

Her heart was pounding. *'Dit moi,'* she shouted to hurry him up.

'C, É, S, A, R.' His pronunciation took ages.

'What, César, did you say?'

She snatched the letter from his hand like a child and scanned through it in no time before jumped up and landed on her high-heeled Jimmy Choo shoes. 'Oh no! I cannot believe it. Oh la la!'

Karim was worried that she was on the verge of madness. He tried to calm her down with no success.

After a period of turbulence when she even ignored the public reaction to her act, she calmed down and composed herself and read in a loud voice. 'You are invited to the night of the César to be presented a lifetime achievement reward.'

'What is the César?' Karim asked in an indifferent tone.

She turned towards him in disgust. How could you not know the César.' She turned into a theatrical actor. 'It is the highest honour a French actor can get. It is equivalent to the American Oscars, if not better.' She stood upright and moved with a seductive gesture as she spun around to depict her delight.

Karim lifted his eyebrows in surprise. 'Anything can happen,' he whispered. He decided to make the best of such a rare moment and advanced towards her, taking the lead in the stumbling steps of a waltz.

Chapter twenty-six

In Preparation for the Great Night

Sandrine's routine had been turned upside down since learning about her up and coming accolade. She was behaving as if she is coming back from the dead; not surprising behaviour for someone who was now a *hasbeen* but who had once been a diva and a recognized star.

She woke up in the morning and had her coffee and more food, half a croissant or less, making sure to weigh it so she kept to her low daily calorie intake.

She skipped her morning drink after vowing to cut down on her alcohol intake. She was busy making phone calls to book appointments with journalists, preparing her speech, booking the hair stylist and the beauty expert. A friend had suggested she had Botox to reduce the depth of the wrinkles in her aging face. She wanted to do it because she would be in the public eye and the eye of her fans. She was investing in everything and anything that could give her a youthful look.

Karim bought a big bundle of French magazines from *Paris Match* to *Point de Vue* that Sandrine ordered him to fetch from the local tabac. She wanted to know who would be attending, what the latest gossip was, whether Catherine

Deneuve was slimmer than her or not, what kind of jewels to wear, and the dress Juliette Binoche would be wearing. So many decisions to make that it was difficult to put then into practice.

Karim was happy witnessing her transformation into a new person by having a new lease on life. He tried to follow her instructions accurately, but her attention to detail drove him mad. Nothing was good enough for her. Most importantly, she needed to dress well for the occasion. She wanted to be Sandrine with 1963 youth and beauty. All of a sudden, the famous haute couture houses sent her dresses to try for the grand party; she had to choose between the French-based, Paris-based designers — Chanel, Yves Saint Laurent and Lanvin. But she paid some attention to the Italian ones such as Dolce & Gabbana and Valentino. The Middle-Eastern haute couture designer Elie Saab have drew her attention since the story about Joan Collins wearing one of his designs at an Oscar party a few years ago.

The unexpected attention lifted her mood and boosted her confidence and she came back to being the well-known diva, the *grand French diva*. Nevertheless, Karim had to suffer her tantrums and unrealistic demands to bring the night of her life to perfection. But he enjoyed the new Sandrine. Since the new-life change Karim spent the majority of his time at her place. He stayed in the spare room in her flat when she was in a pleasant mood. Sometimes she invited him to her room with a glass of champagne or he would lock himself in his room to avoid her explosive and unpredictable mood swings, when hell broke loose. At these times he wished he could escape to the dump of a room that he shared with his fellow countrymen at Belleville. He would find any excuse to leave the apartment for a walk or to make a phone call to his family who were still suffering the atrocious living conditions in the refugee camp. He had no apparent hope of reuniting with them.

Sandrine was aware of his bewildered thoughts and tried to console him.

'Are you okay?' she asked in a soft voice.

'Yes fine,' he said in a strong voice. He was surprised by her rare gentle approach.

'You do not seem to be,' she added in caring tone.

'I am worried about my family.'

'I hope you can reunite with them,' she said the words with hesitation, unsure if she meant them and worried she would lose him.

'I have to go to England.' He gazed at the ceiling, reaching for the sky.

'No, you should not. You are better off in France. I will look after you.' Her voice went from firm to begging.

'Thanks, but French immigration laws are difficult. I don't have residency which would help me to settle in France, so I could claim asylum in the UK. Then I could bring my family.'

She looked at her dog. 'We will be alone soon,' she whispered so that Karim could not hear. The dog walked away as if he was bored with her comment. 'Even you doggy want to abandon me,' she mumbled.

The unexpected closeness between the two made Karim realise how broken-hearted she was. He pitied her for her loneliness and the lack of love in her life. He dared to sit next to her on the designer sofa and tried to reach her. Sandrine extended her hand and came closer which encouraged him to come closer to her. He maintained caution because of her unpredictable behaviour. Her head landed heavily on his chest and her dyed blonde hair was fluttered by the breath from his nostrils. 'Do you like it?' she asked.

'I feel responsible for you and that it is my duty to look after you.'

His statement drew a wide smile on her immaculately lipsticked mouth. 'Do you like me or love me?'

Karim jerked his arms and she felt him go tense.

'Mam, I care for you because I am indebted to you.' His voice was formal but full of masculinity that made her feel safe but equally uncomfortable and insecure.

'Is that all?' she asked as if there was a frog in her throat.

'Well, you are an old lady. The age of my mother.' He uttered the words as if he was sending her to the guillotine.

'Old! Your mother! How dare you?' she shouted at him and pushed his strong chest away.

'Buuut,' he stammered.

'Get out from my sight … out.' She threw a bunch of neatly lined up magazines from the coffee table towards him.

He stood up and headed in haste to the front door having been chased away by Sandrine's fit of shouting and the dog's barking as he responded to his mistress' distress.

Chapter twenty-seven

Life is a Roller Coaster

Karim decided to give Sandrine a miss this time. Her attitude was too much to cope with. Her aggression, clingy behaviour and rude manners repelled him. On the other hand, he struggled to ignore the soft vulnerable side of her character which he'd had the privilege to discover.

Sandrine was clouding his concern about his wife and children. Fadwa had not been in touch with him for a while which was out unusual. He tried relentlessly to make calls to her mobile with no success. Silence was the equivalent to death in a very mad world such as he was living in.

In France, the word refugee comes with a sinister meaning. Nevertheless, it was heaven to reach the West rather than staying in the hellish war zone in Syria. His sleepless nights made him speculate about where his family was, what they were they doing, and if they were alive? Questions without answers. He missed his children, his most precious beings. In the overcrowded room that he shared, he spent the night browsing on his mobile, Googling the latest news in the Middle East as he searched for any trace of his family or relatives or anyone related to him.

Life was becoming more and more difficult. He was unable to find work after the French authorities had responded to the far right movement's notion to control the *foreign invasion*. The French population was dogged by unemployment, financial hardship and the fears of the shrinking French culture in the face of other invading cultures, particularly the Islamic one.

In the middle of his muddled thoughts his phone rang. Karim's hands were shaking in case it was bad news. *Will I answer to hear how my family has been banished?* The heavy snoring from his roommates was louder than his phone ringing.

His shaking hands pressed on the *on* button. An unknown number was depicted on the smartphone screen. The voice was a harsh man who spoke in Arabic. '*Alsalaam Alaykum.*'

Karim cleared his throat with difficulty and responded in feeble voice, '*Salaam.*'

'Are you Karim?' the stranger asked.

'Yes, I am.'

'Your wife and children …' Before the man said anything more Karim fell on the floor. The mobile escaped his weak, tremulous hand. The voice on the other end became distant. '*Allo, allo?*' The harsh masculine voice was replaced by a soft feminine one that he recognised.

'Karim, it's me, Fadwa.' Her words brought him back from death.

He rushed to pick up the phone. 'Darling how are you and the children? Where are you?'

'We are fine and we've been displaced from one camp to another. We have tried to cross the border, but they caught us in Greece.'

'How could you do that without asking me? And where are the kids?' he shouted as he interrupted her.

'They are fine; I am talking from a satellite phone.'

'Swear to God that they are fine.' His voice was so loud that his mates woke from their deep sleep.

'They are fine and they will call you as soon as they get their mobiles back.'

'How did you get the money?'

'I had to sell my mother's jewels. I had them hidden in my bra.'

'How silly you are.'

'What could I do? We want to be with you.'

'Not to worry, darling. I am sorry. I will sort it out.'

'Karim—' Her voice cut off abruptly when the operator said her time was up.

'My time is up,' he whispered. 'I have to raise money for their journey to get my family out of that misery.'

Chapter twenty-eight

No Pride in Time of Need

Karim knocked on so many doors to finance his dreams of a reunion with his family with no glimpse of hope. The French immigration authorities tightened the ring yet again on immigrants. He barely survived on a couple of hundred euros per month. Needless to say after the daily living costs to cover food, rent and bills it was impossible to save money to send to support his family. His income was too small.

As the days went by, he lost hope of finding a job; he spent relentless effort finding a job with a decent salary. It was like a dream. He spent days and days searching without success. He got a few hours of hard labour in the meat market and was rewarded with a pittance.

Once, he found a job in the vegetable market, but the police raided the site looking for illegal workers and searching those who were suspected of having a liaison with extremist organisations. He fled the scene without his day's pay. His only remedy was walking in Paris — it was free. He walked miles and miles along the banks of Seine River, passing the sumptuous Parisian bridges. He strolled in the Bois de Boulogne where he was stopped by prostitutes offering services that he could not afford. He was surprised when a Latino transgender prostitute tried to lure him to her adapted van to service her clients in return of money for sexual favours. Karim entertained the idea of having some fun when he recalled the inauguration of his manhood with a school mate when he was fifteen years old.

'Do you want to have some fun?' the prostitute asked as she approached him with her South American accent. She was wearing tight leggings and a T-shirt with high-heeled shoes. Her make-up seemed to be overdone to attract clients. The silver glitter of the eye shadow matched her cheap style that hinted at the oldest profession ever.

'I can do anything you like for fifty euros.' She gave the quote without the slightest emotion or interest in the young, good-looking man in French in her hard to comprehend Spanish accent.

Karim glanced at her cleavage with immense desire but thought about how he couldn't afford such an adventure and then there were the religious repercussions and prohibitions that surfaced.

'Non merci,' he said in despair.

The night was gloomy, but the days were becoming longer and warmer as summer approached slowly and steadily. Paris had become busier with an enormous number of tourists flocking from all over. All that meant nothing to Karim whose life has been halted since his last failed attempt to escape to the UK.

As he approached his favourite spot by the Seine next to the Pont Neuf, his phone rang. The name Sandrine gave him the creeps. *What does she want? Another problem. He tried to be fair to her. Well she was a senior demented woman and she paid him well besides offering him* some *physical satisfaction.* He answered with a shaky voice. *'Allo.'*

A voice spoke as if it was a prima donna from the Opéra de Paris. *'Bonsoir, c'est* Sandrine La Croix. *Bonsoir.* Is that Karim?' Her tone became less arrogant and mellowed.

He knew she had recognised him. *'Oui.'*

'How are you? I have not heard from you for a while. I was expecting you to come,' she said in a demanding tone.

He was puzzled by her arrogance and ignorance. She had sacked him and humiliated him. 'I thought you sack—'

She interrupted him. 'Good employees should be punctual. I will expect you tomorrow. *Bon nuit.'* She stopped abruptly. 'Do not forget, you should abide by your contract conditions with me or else'. Her authoritarian tone irritated him. 'Please come.' The latter part of her speech was soft and seductive in tone. She hung up without giving him the chance to explain himself.

The shock of her erratic behaviour confused him and he lost his way back home.

At home he tried to sleep with the snoring of his roommates and the smell of humus that they'd had earlier for dinner kept him awake. Then there was the odour of his roommates feet and shoes. He slept dreaming of the reunion with his family. He remembered Haji saying, *"La vie est dur."* He was right; life was difficult.

Chapter twenty-nine

The Night of her Life

Châtelet was the same as it had been for many years. It was quiet but busy. Karim tried to use the cheapest options to reach Sandrine's house from Belleville, either walking or using buses. But not tonight. He coughed up a small fortune for a taxi. His thoughts were focused on Sandrine's reaction to his delay or any other thing she might invent, but he thought more about the pay. The thought of that made him determined to cope with her tantrums and explosive moods. The only way to stop her unpredictable moods was to praise her youthful looks after she underwent a few aesthetic procedures and maybe her talent. He'd been forced to watch many of her films on YouTube and he'd admired her look and acting alike. Since she'd learnt that she had been invited to receive the lifetime achievement at the night of the César, her life had been turned upside down. It was the forerunner to her attending the Cannes film festival to secure some recognition from her fans and maybe from the seventh art industry that could secure her work by meeting producers and directors from France and all over the world.

He recalled one evening when wine played with her head and she was dancing to Édith Piaf's words, *Tu me fait tourner la tête*. She wrapped Karim in her arms and put on in extreme effort to teach him to waltz in a passive manner. While they are dancing she whispered, 'I am happy. I feel I have a new lease on life.'

'I have noticed,' he replied with apparent caution as he waited for her reaction.

'You remind me of when I met an Arab prince in the 1960s. He was as handsome as you are. We spent time at his palace in Saint Tropez in southern France. It seems like yesterday.' She melted in his strong arms and handed control to him despite being a control freak, but perhaps she might have to bend to the wind and submit to her man. She stood upright and continued. 'I will teach you the waltz. I was taught by a dancing master when I played the Queen of France in the late 1960s' epic *La Reine*.' Sandrine was high, not only over the clouds but over the moon and even the stars too when she uttered her words. Karim realised her limited physical ability which impacted her spins and manoeuvres and diminished her balance and slowed his struggling pace. Sandrine stopped and sat on her gilded lounger. 'I need to get prepared,' she said. 'My fans have not seen me for the last thirty years. I should come back in a vengeance.' She pointed to her face and hair. 'Sit down,' she said with a regal gesture.

Karim sat with hesitation, knowing her volatile mood, a landmine, was waiting to be triggered. She approached him like a snake waiting to attack its prey. She pouted her well-painted lips and kissed him. He sucked at her lips with a big appetite. She felt a new chapter of her life had begun. *Was it true or a mirage?* The same question came to Karim's mind.

Chapter thirty

Nuit de César

Paris was preoccupied and obsessed with its baby, the César awards ceremony It was an accolade to every French actor and an honour that comes after the Cannes film festival. The French invited their long lost royalty and substituted them with stars, actors and divas. Haute couture made its choice of the actresses and some of the Parisian socialites to promote their latest designs. This night was crucial to this multi-million industry.

Every actress wanted to be many steps ahead her rival. French cinema treasures its ageing actresses who are appreciated by the French like the old wines, contrary to the American ones who are left on the shelves after age forty something. The artists and the fans flocked to central Paris with the latest designs and various choices of dresses and jewels after suffering the ordeal of passing the immense scrutiny by their fans and colleagues as they waited for the verdict of who was the prettiest, youngest and the most elegant. Sandrine was no different. She felt the pressure of going back after thirty years in the limelight and the public attention. But it was not easy. She spent days crying, shouting and yelling at poor Karim, venting her anger and frustration for not looking as beautiful and youthful as she wanted. Without warning, her mood changed and would oscillate between being angry and abusive to apologetic, much to Karim's astonishment. She had a fight with two journalists who used to be friends. They had volunteered to prepare her speech and she objected to everything they suggested. Karim suggested an Algerian French teacher could help prepare her speech.

'But she is not French,' Sandrine replied.

'She was born in France, like you.' Karim's reply was too heavy for her ears, she disapproved.

Her choice of dress and shoes and the matching handbag was a daunting task to Sandrine and even more so to the stylist whose efforts to convince her to consider the Italian designers rather than the French ones went in despair.

Do Italians have haute couture houses!' Her response lifted the stylist eyebrows.

The high-end cars such as Porsche and Rolls Royce pulled up in front of the Théâtre du Châtelet. It was a stone's throw from Sandrine's address. A car to turn heads was crucial to impress and it was necessary to convince others that she not struggling financially or begging for roles in cinema or TV. The BMW parked in front of the theatre. The festival attendants opened the car door and Sandrine descended showing her well sculpted legs under her black, silver-beaded Chanel dress and Roger Vivier black stiletto-heeled shoes. The steward touched her hand and she wanted to hand her Prada handbag to Karim who was so anxious that he'd had an alcoholic drink at home before they had left to calm his nerves. She had been mentoring Karim for high lifestyle living — how to eat, what and when to talk and finally he had no choice when she chose the colour of his suit. He begged her to buy a cheaper version of the big brand names but she wouldn't budge. Caring for Karim was a great distraction for her troubled soul. Regardless, she forgot about herself and Karim the minute the camera flashes blinded her eyes and it was all *me, me, me.*

The cheers from the fans boosted her adrenaline and she felt ten years younger or more. It reminded her of the sunset Boulevard song, *As If We Never Said Goodbye*, when the limelight mesmerised her and she was worshiped by fans but equally betrayed by them. The song that played in her head was, *You'll Never Know How Much I Miss You*. But she woke up when she was blinded by the cameras flashes which were not as irritating as the 1960s old cameras she was used to coping with. She forgot she was a long-gone star, passe as she was described by the media, even so she wanted her few moments of fame. Karim was baffled by all that attention and curiosity. He was ridden by guilt, having left his family and his country to suffer and now he was in the middle of the limelight, surrounded by glamour. The stewards paid attention to the minute details which were necessary to deal with big egos such as those of the stars or some of them at least. A steward realised Karim's conundrum and his astonishment at accompanying Sandrine La Croix; he was like a lost child looking for his mother. But the steward guided him towards her and instructed him to hold her hand. She gave him a disgusted look with a warning on her forehead for not learning his lesson, that he should walk one step after her and that he should be photographed once or maybe twice, but the rest was for her, her and only her. The intimidation was apparent on Karim's face. She held his hand with a strong grip and significant clinging. Her wet hand sent him a warning and reflected her high level of anxiety. She entered the magnificent belle époque architecture theatre triumphant like an uncrowned queen as she marched along the corridor, ignoring the steward's directions, having been here every year since she was given a César award in 1976. She knew the theatre's plan like the back of her hand. She felt extra honoured by the lifetime achievement which is bestowed once in a lifetime and to very few of her colleagues or rival actors.

She was seated in the front row of the theatre from where she turned to scan the seats in search of familiar faces. The majority of young men and women, actors, producers and directors were unfamiliar but they had heard of her. Some she had heard of or about while she'd been watching TV and very rarely going to watch films in the cinema. Her main target was the older ones who were dropping out like flies. Perhaps she could not recognise them after all the face lifts and Botox and even liposuction. She viewed herself as she'd been in her twenties. The overwhelming emotions took her over and Sandrine was reliving her heydays, without taking any notice of poor Karim who was overwhelmed by his alien surroundings.

Sandrine woke from a half-dream, half-reality trance to a voice she did not welcome.

'Sandrine, I never expected to see you.'

Sandrine turned to see what made her wake up to a live nightmare. Claudette was trouble wherever she went, at least from Sandrine's point of view. Sandrine answered with a fake smile.

'*Bonsoir.* You must have not been reading newspapers or watching the media, I am here to receive the lifetime achievement. I am a talented actor.' Sandrine words hit Claudette like a bolt of lightning.

'Really!' Claudette replied in a sarcastic tone.

'Of course and what about you? What are you doing here?'

'You haven't read about my nomination for my film role?'

Her statement was a dagger in the heart. *How come that bitch gets all these roles.*

Claudette guessed what she is thinking. 'Oh, you have a toy boy now. Yes, he is young and handsome. What about the French men? Have they disappeared? You have your import from abroad.'

Sandrine felt the insult heavily and for the first time she felt Karim's humiliation could hurt her and diminish her ego. She was about to stand up and hit Claudette. With self-control and restraint Sandrine contained herself. 'Love and kindness are out of your scope. Something you do not know. And I don't expect you to. Now, move from here or I will make you a laughing stock. Now shoo!' she said.

Claudette rushed to the other side of the row in a hurry stumbling as she went and escaping Sandrine's sardonic smile with a facial expression impersonating the devil.

The ceremony commenced with nominations of the winners who raised their heads in pride while the losers hid their heads. Sandrine was shaking like a leaf. It was her day; she had waited all her life for this glory. She did not recognise the names of the nominees until her contemporary fellow actor with whom she had played on the big screen and enjoyed sexual encounters, Joel, announced her name. She was glued to her seat, but Karim asked her politely and softly to go. He planted a kiss on her cheek that gave her the energy to stand. She walked with weak steps, reaching the stage with delay, as if fashionably late as she got into her diva mode. She gazed at the lights piercing her eyes, entertained by the noise of the audience whose excitement to see a long-gone superstar, well-known for her beauty, talent and bad temper, was apparent.

She bowed lightly to the spectators and started her well-rehearsed speech. She greeted the César panel and thanked them for the ceremony recognition. 'There is nothing greater than being missed by fans. I miss you dearly. It am overwhelmed; I am not prepared for such an event. It is beyond my ability. I love to …' Sandrine's speech came to a standstill. She could not speak the words that even Karim had learnt by heart. He tried to prompt her, but he was too far away. A laugh came from the crowd; it became infectious and spread among the spectators. Sandrine could not handle the situation and left her few minutes of fame, and ignored her trophy. She marched out of the podium engulfed by anger and embarrassment.

Karim rushed to her and wrapped his arms around her and hurried her to the door as he forced his way through the middle of the curious crowd, who were eager to know what was going on. He did his best to avoid the approaches of journalists and flashes from photographers. A car came closer and he shoved her inside as if she was a sack of potatoes. He lay her down the newly polished leather seat with its strong smell. He asked the driver to go ahead, not knowing if it was a taxi or a private car. All that mattered was to save Sandrine from embarrassment.

The driver obliged with minimal protest and out of pity for the old weak woman. He had been waiting to pick one of the celebrities who was appearing later in the night.

Karim carried her and marched up the steps to her flat. She was sobbing in a hysterical way. 'I am done. I lost my last chance. It will be a scandal.' Her words were mixed with harrowing sobs.

'Just relax and try to sleep or shall I call the doctor?'

'No need for a doctor. Please stay with me. I need you.' Her begging was a novelty to him.

'But ...' he answered with a puzzled frown.

'I have never ever begged anyone before. Please do not make me.'

'No need to.' He came closer to her and held her hand. She pulled him towards her with unexpected strength. 'Good night,' he said.

Chapter thirty-one

Convalescence after the Scandal

Within a few months after the Césargate or Sandrinegate as it had been called by the French gossip media, Sandrine became a recluse and avoided even walking the dog at the local park as well as shopping. She was increasingly dependent on Karim to do the everyday chores. He moved in to live with her when she increased his pay substantively. He slept in the room adjacent to her bedroom and occasionally he slept in Sandrine's bed when she was in a good mood. She had begun visiting her psychotherapist more frequently, eager to deal with her anger outbursts and her severe anxiety, hoping it would resolve years of accumulated anger, frustration and disappointment in a few sessions. The therapy outcome did not result in less tantrums or episodes of outrage, but they were not directed at Karim. Since the César mishap Sandrine's self-confidence and esteem had hit rock bottom with a significant increase in her anxiety and low moods. She became highly dependent on Karim who coped with her behaviour willingly and lovingly to everybody's surprise. No one could believe the independent, hard-hearted Sandrine had become so soft, needy and clingy towards Karim. She started to have flashbacks from that night that her private psychiatrist diagnosed as Post Traumatic Stress Disorder. Sandrine explained the psychiatric diagnosis to Karim.

'It is the trauma of that night that causes the flashbacks, nightmares and reliving the incident,' she said as she sobbed in his arms.

Karim thought that as he was a war survivor he too had probably suffered of all those symptoms.

'I know you will say you survived a dreadful, bloody war and I asked my psychiatrist about that. He emphasised the vulnerability of the victim rather than the enormity of the event,' she said as she caressed his soft hair and counted the premature his grey hairs to give herself the excuse to be pampered as if she was sick.

He stared at the decorated, white-classical round ceiling medallion as he thought about the horror that he had lived through in his native Syria. The images of dead bodies and wounded children were so intrusive that he shouted. He was concerned that the images were of his wife and children, dead and mutilated.

'No, please not,' he cried then burst into tears. He stood up and moved away from her bed, and rushed to the door to hide his tears. He was not supposed to show others anything than a stiff upper lip and macho character. Sandrine was very sensitive and she transformed from a feeble, helpless old women to a lively, strong one. She caught him by the main door and prevented him from leaving,

'Darling, talk to me. I am here. I have always been the whinger and the complainer. I know you lead a hard life, but trying to bottle it up is harmful.' She caressed his scalp gently, touching his curly, well-greased hair as she tried to reach his cheeks without success. He was taller than her. He bent his body until they were cheek to cheek.

She walked him to the living room and sat on the Louis XIV sofa.

'Darling would you see a mental health professional. I have spent a significant part of my income and time on psychiatrists and psychotherapists,' she whispered as she caressed his hair.

'I bet you would be just as qualified as any one of them, if not better.' He laughed cheerfully.

'*Bien sûr.* I paid the bastards a fortune and here I am alone with no job, no family and the therapist is enjoying his yacht in Saint Tropez.' They laughed loudly.

'Fools live off the mad. It is an Arabic saying.' He giggled to her slight discomfort.

Karim realised his comment might not sit well with her. He thought he was in hot water and got ready for her usual abuse but to his surprise, she glanced thoughtfully at his face and pulled the silk-covered, duck-feather cushion and threw it at his face with a huge laugh. Karim threw it back and feathers flew everywhere.

'I haven't laughed for so long. Summer is almost here and I long for the seaside in southern France. Have you been there?' she asked with a seductive gesture imitating Brigette Bardot in *Dieu Créa la Femme. film*

'Never, I've only seen it on films and photos.'

'Shall we go?' Her tone was enthusiastic.

'How could Sandrine La Croix accompany a poor Syrian refugee?'

'The poor Syrian refugee makes her laugh.' She laughed even louder.

'So I am better than your psychiatrist.'

'A hundred times.' He held her hands with a strong grip and they headed to the bedroom.

Chapter thirty-two

On the Way to the Côte d'Azur

The travel was not planned according to Sandrine's ever-strict regime. Karim booked two tickets on the TGV train to Saint-Raphaël and then a car to Saint-Tropez. He found a budget hotel and complained how expensive it was.

'How much per night?'

'A hundred euros for both of us.'

Sandrine laughed loudly. 'It must be a shitty place'

'What do you mean? This could feed a family for a while back home.'

'I know, dear, but this is France and the Côte d'Azur too. I used to stay with friends in their villa at Ramatuelle my favourite part of Saint Tropez, but I had a clash with Juliette, a friend who I have alienated myself from since she befriended Claudette. They are bitches. Thus I have been staying at the Château de la Messardière hotel since.'

'How much a night?'

'About five hundred euro or so.'

Karim was gobsmacked. The price was a jaw dropper.

Sandrine giggled. 'Don't worry, I do get discounts. I am a walking advertisement. I will call and book.' She dialled the number from her landline. Her tone had changed to the authoritarian diva.

'Here she goes again; the good old Sandrine,' Karim whispered.

'You said something?' she asked in a suspicious tone.

'No, no.' He was scared to reveal his thoughts.

'Voila, we have a deal. There is always a silver lining. The night of the César drama has paid off. We have got a deal. The price is heavily discounted.'

'What about me?'

'Of course. Everyone wants to meet you.'

'Me?' he exclaimed.

'Yes you. You took some of the limelight from me, darling.' She uttered the words tinted with jealousy.

Karim felt reassured that she was back on track. She asked for her white wine and drank it with impatience rather than having her lunch of salad Niçoise with the lowest calories possible. Karim jumped at the opportunity to put his point forward. 'You said that the psychiatrist asked you to be careful with your drinking.'

'My drink is not your business,' she replied in an angry and abrupt tone embedded with defence.

'I know dear, let's try to eat something; I am starving and you must be hungry.'

She fancied the idea of facing the world after a few months of self-imposed isolation since the night of the Césars. 'Let's book at Maxims,' she replied submitting to his demand.

'Oh no, small portions are hardly enough to satisfy my hunger. Do you remember when we went there? I had to eat like this … or do that … all rules and regulations.'

Sandrine smiled showing her nicely whitened teeth. 'Do you remember when we went there and you asked to have fast food afterwards?' she said and to his astonishment and she giggled.

'I was embarrassed to eat. I had to follow your instructions and be scrutinised by other clients and even the media afterwards.'

'Of course, what do you expect when you accompany Sandrine?' She posed like a model.

Karim came closer to her and touched her hand. 'May I suggest something?'

'What?'

'Let's go somewhere else.'

'Where?'

'I know a Lebanese restaurant in Belleville. They serve delicious Middle-Eastern plates.'

The last words landed like a rock on her head.

'Mais non.' Her answer was assertive.

'Oui. It is a new experience and you will never forget it. I want to invite you. The man should pay for his woman.' He said his piece in a strong masculine tone.

His words gave her warmth and protection that she had never felt with all the men she had associated with in the past. She wished to stick by her man for once.

'Let's go.'

Her answer gobsmacked Karim.

Chapter thirty-three

Break at the Côte d'Azur

Summer on the French Rivera is synonymous with beauty, light, lovely weather and glamour. The rich and famous and the A listers from all over the world flock to the clear blue sky and beaches and lovely mistral wind, a necessary refresher to the heat of the higher temperatures associated with the golden rays of the sun. Women walk with pride, showing off the latest fashion trends from bikinis, designer evening dresses, day clothes and jewels. Men are no less modest in showing off their luxurious cars and watches.

A Peugeot car snaked towards Ramatuelle (God's mercy) in Arabic as the Arabs o called Saint Tropez the (*Jabal Al Kom*) or top of mountain in Arabic when they stayed for a short époque of history. The car sped to the Château de Messardière Hotel. It was coming from Saint Raphaël and passing through the centre of Saint Tropez. The car stopped in front of the hotel. Karim exited wearing a T-shirt and jeans. Sandrine's had protested that he was too casual. She wore a Chanel yellow-chiffon, fluffy dress and a matching yellow hat. She had complained all the way from St Raphaël about the long journey from Paris to Saint Tropez and about Karim's bad choice of train seats despite them being in first class and then she had complained about the Uber rather than a proper rental car.

'I should not listen to you. I have always booked with a limousine car company,' she said in an angry tone.

'But they are dear, and it is the same service,' he said knowing Sandrine was not as affluent as she pretended to be, having not worked for the last thirty years.

The hotel manager was waiting for her. She had insisted that Karim call him as soon as they reached St Raphaël. Edmund was a forty-something Frenchman wearing a smoking suit and well-polished shoes. He was wiping sweat drops from his forehead in the warm weather. As he approached the car Sandrine extended her hand, which he touched gently with his rough lips as he kissed it. He revived in her the good old days of romanticism and chivalry.

The other servants were waiting for her and she felt more appreciated than in previous years. Karim was ignored by everyone including Sandrine who was enjoying the attention and feeling like a princess surrounded by her entourage. The younger generation of staff learnt from the older ones who she was — her films and her likes and dislikes during her regular summer visits. The management was over the moon, Sandrine attracted publicity to the hotel despite rooms being reserved one year ahead, but she was still in the limelight after her César mishap with its infamous attention. That's what it was all about in such a society. Appearance was all that mattered.

Sandrine realised that she had left out Karim, and she turned and used her ordering military voice to address him. 'Come with me, dear; let the porters carry the suitcases.' The luggage comprised of four suitcases with Sandrine's clothes that would keep her going for a few months yet she was only staying for three weeks.

They reached the suite which was a complimentary upgrade from hotel management. She opened her mouth wide when she saw the luxury of the place. It had improved her since she began frequenting the hotel in the early 1990s. There was lavish history behind it; it was a real château built in the 19th Century. The room overlooked the vast green hills and the swimming pool. She took a deep breath of the wind coming through the window. The porter Eduardo appeared and Sandrine handed a tip to the young man who was used to receiving fat tips from rich clients.

Karim pulled a face; he was not used to this kind of extravaganza. 'It is too much of a tip. It is my whole day's wage at the meat market,' he said. She shrugged and reminded him that it is not his business.

She sat on the fauteuil beside the coffee table where there was a spectacular view of the landscape, and ignored his remarks. She asked Karim to open the small fridge. 'They always stock it with my favourite white wine,' she said.

He poured a glass for her. She had a few sips and realised that he had not helped himself.

'What is the matter? Won't you have a drink with me?'

'Too early.'

'It's never too early in Saint Tropez.' Sandrine stood up and sighed. 'I am going to rest and prepare myself for the big job.'

'I thought you were on holiday.'

'In my career, business is always business. You never retire from a diva's job.' She giggled and went to the bathroom. He smiled. *She is coming back from the dead.* Karim sat in despair, loaded with guilt. *How can I lead such a life with my family suffering?* He searched for his smartphone in his trouser pocket and dialled What's App, but it was difficult to get a connection. It was then that he heard an irritated voice from the bedroom. 'Karim, can you come and rub my back please?'

'The diva is always a diva,' he said aloud.

After they had rested they decided to go for a walk in the hills, where the views of Ramatuelle and Pampelonne Beach were amazing. 'We will visit the town and Pampelonne Beach where I have been invited to the VIP club and of course, Club 55 and maybe Hotel de la Ponche.'

'Should we?' he replied with astonishment.

'We have to. It is a game and you must know how to play it. It is where the A listers hang out.'

'But you are different.'

'Yes, but not long ago, I was unwell and I have confused my psychiatrists with my diagnosis, let alone the treatment. I think finding a purpose in life is my main problem. I have seen life in a different perspective since I met you. You have picked me up … *merci.*' She came closer to him.

*A diva is always a div*a.

Chapter thirty-four

It is a Holiday

Time was passing fast because it was fun. Sandrine herded Karim to downtown Saint Tropez which reminded him of the old houses in Damascus. They refreshed his pain about his wounded country. Sandrine suggested lunch at Club 55; she explained that it was where you could meet actors, directors, producers and journalists.

'Social media is the new way forward and since we started your Twitter, Facebook and Instagram, the younger generation have started to take notice of you'. Karim kept repeating his mantra to her but it fell on deaf ears. She was old school and would continue to be. You can't teach an old dog a new trick.

Despite her deliberate disappearance from public life, she was still remembered by the older generation.

While Sandrine and Karim were finding their way to a table in the café they came across young girls who were whispering and giggling among themselves. Sandrine smiled with triumph and whispered to Karim. 'They know me.' She tapped her hair which was actually a wig, and there were multi layers of make-up on her face. Karim fancied the beautiful young girls in their prime and reciprocated with a smile. One of them darted her eyes to their table. Then she came closer with her smartphone and prepared to take a photo.

'Sorry, I do not take photos with fans.' Sandrine ushered her away.

'Pardon madame, I am an artist and the gentleman's face is photogenic.' She ignored Sandrine and turned to Karim. 'Monsieur, I have a project and would like to take photos of you.'

He looked at Sandrine with terrified eyes. She was fuming.

The girl took a few photos without permission.

'You should work in media.' She uttered in admiration.

'Do you mean I should work like a model?' His tone was full of pride as he displayed his masculinity to the young girls.

Sandrine was about to explode and tried to stand up to create a scene, until a familiar voice stopped her.

'*Bonjour* Sandrine.' It was a harsh masculine voice with a distinctive Parisian accent. She turned her head to see a seventy-something French man with pronounced wrinkles and grey receding hair, wearing designer shorts and a T-shirt that exposed part of his sagging stomach. *Is that Roger? Look what life has done to a handsome sexy man.* He directed a few films for her and they were in love. He left his wife and children to be with her, but she was not ready to have a relationship nor was she willing to have children to her immense regret later on. Roger advanced towards her and kissed her cheeks three times according to the French etiquette while avoiding touching the multi layers of make-up over her cheeks. She asked him to sit down, forgetting or consciously not introducing him to Karim who felt embarrassed by her behaviour. Sandrine gazed at the lines and wrinkles around Roger's eyes and on his forehead. There was a trace of his long-gone good looks.

'How are you doing?' Roger asked her in a tone full of fondness.

'I am what I am. I am well and you?' she responded in a flat voice. 'Actually, I am fine now that I have seen you,' she added.

'Tell me how is life?' he said.

'As you see, I am trying to put my foot on the ladder again.' She made a move as if she was the lead dancer at the Moulin Rouge.

They chatted for twenty minutes before she turned to Karim who sat silently chewing his humiliation. 'Oh, may I introduce you to Karim, Roger.' She uttered the words fast and indifferently as she continued her reminiscence of the old days and films. The session was long and went on for couple of hours. Karim did not utter a single word, nor he was allowed to. He observed Sandrine becoming tipsy. She was trying to maintain her self-restraint with difficulty. If she became drunk all hell would break loose. She started to talk about her adventures with Roger during her youth and gave away far too much information.

'Do you remember when we shot the film in the Amazon in South America, Roger?' she asked as she touched his beard with her forefinger.

'How could I forget. Only if I get dementia. I will never forget it. It was the happiest time of my life.'

She laughed in a relaxed manner. 'Oh la la! And when the shooting went ahead after the mayor wanted to speak to me and I refused to be nice to him, he banned us from filming on the basis of indecent behaviour in a strict Catholic country. The production was at a standstill until I phoned the president of Peru who granted us permission. He was a big fan of mine.'

'And he sacked the poor mayor.' Roger laughed loudly and his speech was incoherent because of the effect of the wine on his empty stomach.

'But sure, it was Sandrine la Croix.' She uttered the words with immense pride, and raised her glass in a grand show to attract the café customer's attention.

Karim's head was rolling like a yoyo between the two of them having been ignored by both until Sandrine realised. 'Pardon, Roger was the director and producer of the majority of my films'. She finished the latter part of her sentence in English. She turned to Roger. 'This is Karim.' She pointed at him without eye contact. She had forgotten that she had already made the introduction.

Roger gave Karim a look full of disgust. 'Hello,' he said half-heartedly then turned to her, chit-chatting and sharing old memories. The afternoon passed and dinner time approached.

'Pardon chérie. I have a business dinner tonight and I need to get ready.' He left after saying goodbye. Sandrine was ecstatic either from the alcohol or memories but equally annoyed at losing Roger's attention. Karim was despondent. She looked at him and realised that he was unhappy.

'Darling this world is like that. You have to get used to it'. She touched his cheek fondly, coping with his prickly beard.

'He insulted me,' he said in a quiet voice.

'No, this is the way people from my generation behave. I think he was jealous of you. He used to adore me, but I rejected him.' She gave a seductive pout and touched his head.

'Why?'

'I have always distanced myself from others; the closer they come to me, the further away I push them.' She tousled his black hair.

'Let's leave.' She called the waiter for the bill.

They strolled in the alleyways where Sandrine was greeted by boutique owners. She did some shopping — a beach dress with a hat was mandatory in Saint Tropez. She told Karim that they had to enjoy every moment.

Yes, life is too short.

'And you have to squeeze every minute of joy out of it, but it is easier said than done.' Her words felt genuine to Karim.

They spent days at the small town and at her favourite Pampelonne Beach. Sandrine was there to show herself to the world. Ready to declare, *I am here.* People were not avoiding her as she imagined they might. She felt the reward of being receptive to others, reciprocating their acceptance and occasionally kindness.

She sat at Cap 21 Les Murènes restaurant, having a lunch of salad and white wine which was more than filling for Sandrine's tiny stomach, but it is not satisfying for Karim's healthy appetite and he scrutinised the menu for the non-existent halal meat or the other vegetarian options. He was pleased to find a kebab shop run by Moroccan immigrants in a forgotten corner of the old city. It advertised halal meat and was frequented by immigrants and a few Middle-Eastern tourists.

'They make a delicious kebab,' he said.

She looked at him with a smile to please a child, not willing to reveal her thoughts and opinions of how non-classy those people were. But she could not hide her feelings towards Karim.

'Yes? We will go if that makes you happy.' She had never said that to a man nor felt the need to please one.

More days passed by that were spent between cafés, restaurants and the beach. While she was contemplating the blue sea, his fit young body was chasing the waves that reminded him of when he swam at Latakia the principal port city of Syria. It was the same kind of sea.

She woke from her daydream to a voice she loathed. 'Bonjour Sandrine, How are you?'

She traced the voice to see a body wearing a bra and a skirt and showing a wrinkly stomach and saggy boobs. The face was hidden behind dark Chanel sunglasses and large straw hat. 'I did not expect you here.'

It was Claudette. Forever the thorn in her side.

'Likewise. What brought you here?' Sandrine said avoiding eye contact.

'You know I own a big villa at Ramatuelle.' She gave Sandrine the signal that she was still a successful actress with more than enough money.

'Well, I thought you had sold it after you declared bankruptcy,' Sandrine hissed with contempt.

'Darling, you've been a recluse. Haven't you heard of the TV series I am making? I've got a contract from subscription channels.'

'Really, and what role you are doing, a grandmother one?' The last word was emphasised by Sandrine.

'I do not think at this age you can get a young girl's role, knowing you are older than me. At least, I am not in denial.'

Before Sandrine's inner volcano erupted, Karim appeared from the sea on a rescue mission. He approached the women and greeted them with caution. Sandrine held his hand proudly. 'My Karim, chérie.' Claudette examined his naked torso thoroughly with an expert's eyes. Sandrine deliberately pulled him towards forcefully and gave him a bouche-à-bouche kiss.

Claudette was fuming. Sandrine recorded a win as Claudette left in haste without saying goodbye.

'What is she doing here?' Karim asked in a loud voice.

'I have posed the same question.' She fiddled indifferently with her hat as she watched the defeated Claudette depart in shame. She celebrated her triumph with a smirk.

At that moment her mobile rang. She was looking for it in her beach bag when Karim came to her rescue and handed the phone to her.

'Allo Roger, nice to hear from … yes … oh yes, of course. I will be tonight'. She ended the call and screamed in happiness. 'I am invited tonight.'

'Where?' Karim asked eagerly.

'It seems promising.'

'What is promising?'

'The secretory of the production company has invited me to the annual party at the Villa Ephrussi de Rothschild.'

'I do not understand.' Karim could not hide his bewilderment from his bronzed face.

There is an annual party where the seventh art stakeholders meet to finalise contracts for films and TV series. And when the CEO of the biggest TV production company invites you in person, there is only one meaning.'

'What is that?' he asked with naivety on his face.

'I have been selected for a role in a production.' She sat cross-legged showing her well sculpted calves.

'And where is that place?' he asked.

'It is an old villa, actually a château at Saint-Jean-Cap-Ferrat built by the Rothschild banking family early last century. And before she could continue, a middle-aged fan approached and took off his hat.

'Nice to see mam; we would like to see you on the screen again.' He took off his hat out of respect and admiration.

'Indeed. You will. I can assure you, you will.' Sandrine printed a big smile of triumph on her tiny lips.

Chapter thirty-five

Night out in Saint Tropez

The days passed quickly. Sandrine and Karim had the same routine of spending the day on the beach, shopping, wining and dining. Numerous invitations were showered upon Sandrine and the recent interest of the media refreshed memories of her fans, media and also producer's attention.

But the invitation she was looking forward to was the one at the VIP nightclub where the rich and famous flocked to the communal or VIP part of the nightclub. The directors and producers gathered with the wealthy businessmen who were interested in making a profit from the cinema and TV industry. Roger had hinted at the possibility of nominating her for a major role on screen after an informal chat with the future production company CEO Monsieur Rumley at the annual Villa Rothschild party.

The arts business relies enormously on publicity and what Sandrine did recently would be sufficient to make her known to the younger generation and revive the memories of the older ones.

Also, with the help of Karim, re-introducing her via social media had helped too.

She was preparing herself by drinking less alcohol with some struggle, eating healthily and exercising. She had been paying endless visits to her wardrobe, trying to pick the right dress or dragging Karim to the Saint Tropez posh boutiques where the haute couture designers showed their latest clothing designs. Sandrine was more inclined towards the older generation of designers while Karim's advice was more for the new ones, but most of all he was keen on decent dresses that didn't show arms or cleavage. 'Do you want me to wear a burka too?' she would ask in response to his suggestions.

'No, just elegant decent dress. I don't want other men to look at your body.' He showed his protectionist attitude towards her.

She laughed with satisfaction. She was wanted and loved. She ended up choosing a young unknown Middle-Eastern designer. 'What do you think of this dress, Karim?' She showed him a dress by the Lebanese designer Elie Saab that showed a great proportion of her arms and cleavage.

'It is elegant,' he said sarcastically.

'And decent.' She laughed, calming his hidden protest and agreed to pay for the dress. She was not conscious of her aging saggy body and didn't care about showing some parts of it.

Everything was planned to perfection: her make-up, her dress and the blonde wig, covering the thin hair battered by time and studio lights. She took the initiative and chose a smoking or tuxedo suit for Karim, with a matching bow tie. She paid great attention to the colour coordination. Karim realised that smart casual was the answer but her dress code was the 1960s style. It was reminiscent of the good old days.

The night arrived and the hotel booked a limousine to take them to the VIP room at the nightclub situated by the seafront of Saint Tropez. It rivalled the VIP room in Paris. French and foreign celebrities were in abundance.

Karim wanted to sit next to the driver who pulled a face in disgust

'*Allez,* come next to me,' she rebuked him as she asked him to open the door and sit next to her.

The car drove towards town passing the listed centre and the seafront packed with tourists and locals alike. There were walkers and older locals playing pétanque or going home to dine. Her memories took her back to the days when Saint Tropez was a village and not have been spoilt by commercialism and tourism until Brigitte Bardot's famous or infamous film brought the fishing village to the tourism map. Life went by in a flash. It is like yesterday.

The car reached its destination, which seemed modest from the outside, but not the inside. The loud music and the lights and too many of the younger generation annoyed Sandrine. She regretted allowing herself to compete with young girls which was an opportunity for Karim to indulge in eye candy.

Roger came and made a wolf whistle. 'Oh la la! You are gorgeous.'

'*Merci,*' she responded in a seductive tone much to Karim's annoyance.

He nodded to Karim; the two men obviously did not like each other. He led the way to the private VIP section of the club where Sandrine met new faces including actors, actresses and directors. But, more pleasantly she met the old generation she had worked with over the years. They exchanged memories and news: some had died while others continued to work and a few had given up and retired.

Roger poured pink champagne into crystal flutes and proposed a toast, 'To the revival of the coming star Sandrine.'

She was happily shocked and expecting a major role in a film because he had addressed the speech to her. 'Chérie, we are starting a TV series similar in style to Netflix but in French and I want you to be in it.'

'*Oui,* why not.' She tried to hide her excitement and hide her desperation.

Karim kissed her.

'You are a good omen in my life,' she said.

The oysters and Champagne that were offered generously appalled Karim. He detested that kind of food even though his stomach was rumbling of hunger. He was looking forward to a kebab.

All of a sudden cheers was heard in the distance. 'Hello everyone,' Claudette said as she walked steadily despite her swollen ankles battered by chronic arthritis. She tried to hide her shuffling gait. She was wearing a short, pink Versace dress with matching handbag and shoes. She was parading on the stage in competition with girls much younger than her, and kissing everyone in the room and hugging Roger, showering him with praise and glorifying his masterpiece films, even the unsuccessful ones. She deliberately ignored Sandrine.

Later, she turned towards her and gave her a cursory glance as she examined her figure, clothes, accessories and make-up. 'Hi, I am surprised to see you here; it is an exclusive place,' she said and turned her back on Sandrine.

Sandrine felt the need to escape, but Karim's warm, strong hand held hers firmly as he encouraged her to answer.

'A listers, bring glamour to any place, Claudette.' Sandrine grabbed the opportunity to annoy her even further. 'Karim, darling, shall we dance?' He was embarrassed, not used to dancing; he stepped on her feet, then let her take the lead.

Claudette gulped more alcohol that gave her the courage to approach Karim. 'Will you dance with me?' Sandrine looked daggers at her and Karim did not know what to do, until Roger spoke.

'Ladies and gentleman, let's toast the star who will honour our screens after long absence … Sandrine!' The cheers of a drunken crowd filled the air of the private sector of the nightclub. The cheers saved Claudette a huge reprisal from Sandrine.

'Congratulations. I know we don't get on well, but we will have to live with each other,' Claudette hissed in Sandrine's ear.

'Why?' Sandrine looked away to minimize Claudette's statement.

'Because you and I are the main protagonists in that TV series.'

'No way!' Sandrine's angry voice attracted attention, but Roger intervened in time. He rushed to rescue the situation. 'I will never act with her,' Sandrine hissed in his ear.

'The role is written for both of you. After all, you have acted together before,' he reminded her of the old films she had shared with Claudette.

'She is a nightmare to work with.'

'You will have to put up with her. The series is a follow-up to the 1960s film we shot in South America.'

'No way. I cannot deal with her arrogance and rudeness.'

Roger produced a piece of paper and a fountain pen and started writing much to Sandrine's shock.

'Wow!' she said as her mouth opened wide in astonishment and disbelief. She could not believe her eyes. She was looking hopelessly for her reading glasses to check what he had written.

Roger watched her face. 'Yes, my dear. This is the average pay nowadays,' he said in a proud and winning tone.

'Well, I will consider it then. Even coping with bitches comes with a reward.'

He smirked.

Karim was watching from a distance in bewilderment.

'A miraculous U-turn of luck,' Sandrine mumbled.

Chapter thirty-six

Back to Paris

The Parisians were struggling with the post-holiday blues. The masses were dispirited after having the whole month in other areas of France and abroad. They were unhappy going back to their usual daily routines.

Sandrine signed a contract to start the new TV series about two senior women struggling to come in terms with the ageing process, their relationships and their sex lives.

Across the Atlantic, a TV series executed by Jane Fonda and the likes of Sandrine's generation followed suit. Nevertheless, the French treasured their cinema divas and were ever loyal to watch their production rather than that of their Anglo-Saxon counterparts. The French were keener on the TV set than social media and did not want to pay subscription fees for certain TV channels.

Sandrine got herself into a rigid daily routine and would not deviate from it for any reason.

The shooting day started early in the morning. Sandrine woke at 5 a.m., full of energy with a cup of espresso prepared by Karim. He woke earlier to recite his morning prayers as he thought about his family even though he was immersed in the novel, magical and hard world of television. And it was his escapism. Then they prepared themselves for the day. They took the studio car and headed to the studio or to an outside location if that was required. Sandrine re-discovered herself as an actor, a woman and human being too. Her self-confidence was boosted when Karim held her hand and provided her with reassurance. She continued to argue with the director and producers about the slightest details but more with Claudette. The competition was fierce between the two divas, starting with performance quality, proportions of each one's role, whose name came first, dresses, shoes, accessories, the choice of male actors and on it went. The two divas arguments escalated to angry disputes and even to a catfight that was interpreted well on the silver screen. The plot had been written for two famous passé actresses fighting to spend the later part of their lives performing on theatre and ending up sharing the same accommodation. The series succeeded in a fiercely competitive market of satellite channels, as well as Netflix and Apple.

One day in the studio café, Sandrine asked Karim to bring her a glass of white wine with her lunch that consisted of salad and roast chicken. At that moment Claudette entered.

'Hi,' she said. 'You were not too bad today in the morning shoot,' Claudette's tone was clearly sarcastic.

'Really?! Well, your acting skills have improved significantly.' Sandrine stared at the food in front of her.

'If you remember when I was the lead and you were only a co-star in *L'amour Éternelle*, I tried to teach you how to act,' Claudette spat and gave a smirk.

'Certainly, you are much older than me,' said Sandrine. Claudette did not take her remark kindly. She stood up and threw the script on the floor. I cannot work with you,' she shouted.

Sandrine threw down the gauntlet by pulling herself from her comfy chair with twenty-something girl energy. 'You are miserable.'

'What about you. You are a psychopath' The high-pitched voices filled the small studio café with the gathering crew of actors and technicians. Flashes went off from crew and journalist's cameras and smartphones. The only happy person was the producer who turned to Roger as he tried to mediate between the two stars. 'Leave them alone,' the producer said. 'The longer they carry on, the better.' His laugh showed his excitement as he watched the cat fight and imagined the publicity it would generate tomorrow.

'What do you mean. They could kill each other?' Roger responded in an anxious voice.

'Even better. It is publicity for the show and it reflects the storyline.'

'How come?'

'You will see everything tomorrow in the news and social media ... actually tonight.'

Roger's face went red. 'That is not ethical.'

'Come on, neither you nor I would have chosen them if it wasn't for their recent fights and scandals.'

Roger advanced on the women. '*Arrêtez* ladies. Stop it.' His pleas went in vain.

The women were eventually pulled apart and the director decided to have a shooting break until the two stars settled down. Karim had been running errands for Sandrine and when he came back he went straight to her room.

'Where are you when I need you? Chasing the young technicians?' Her voice was full of rage.

'What do you mean? I went to buy what you asked me for and the young girl you are referring to has stopped talking to me since you told her off.'

Sandrine glanced at her face in the mirror. The Botox might have softened the lines but her wrinkles were recounting stories from years gone by. She turned to Karim with tears in her eyes.

'Darling, I do not know why I lash out at people. My therapist thinks I suffer a personality disorder. They call it borderline. I have read about it and I cannot recall having any problems such as abuse or neglect in my early childhood. My parents were a post-war couple who were not well off, but they provided me and my sister with love and care. They were distant and aloof but it was the norm for that generation. Fame is a curse. I wish I was an ordinary housewife with a husband and children.'

Karim, hugged her and patted her back. She hugged him back. 'I needed that. Oh God, how much I miss it.'

Chapter thirty-seven

The Fruits of Success

The TV series went from success to success. The sales were beyond the producers and the production companies' expectations and passed from the traditional Francophile market to the English one and beyond.

The conflicts and fights between the two divas were entertaining not only to the silver-haired audience but to the younger ones also. Sandrine's boosted morale and confidence resulted in the resurrection of a diva. A star was born. She negotiated an extraordinary deal regarding her wages. But most of all it was higher than Claudette.

One of the veteran, semi-retired cameramen who had worked in parallel with Sandrine in her heydays said to the camera crew, 'it is like she is coming back from the dead.' A make-up artist commented, 'She thrives on others like a vampire.'

Sandrine meant her ongoing quarrels with Claudette to continue because they gave her drive and enabled her to thrive. Nevertheless, it was vital and rejuvenating and reviving for both and enhanced the spirt of competition. Sandrine's new discipline drove her away from Karim, her dog and more importantly her drinking. She became careful, watching her alcohol intake and more eating healthily.

'Is Claudette slimer, younger or better looking than me?' she bombarded poor Karim with this question repeatedly.

'You are far superior,' he answered often. And he kept answering her in this way as if he was on automatic pilot.

The cat fights between Sandrine and Claudette attracted the attention of the gossip magazines too. It was a novelty in the Gallic press. Who would use the make-up room first? Which changing room had the prime position? And then there was the best-dress designer competition. The two actresses spent a fortune on their clothes. They changed the old studio system when the film producers footed the bill for all their expensive clothes, make-up, shoes and even waxing. To their surprise and shock, it is not the same anymore. The producers wanted a rapid gain. The shooting schedule was followed strictly. The girls were reprimanded on a few occasions after short interruptions and delays in shooting and a significant loss in the production budget. The producers recuperated their gains fast regardless.

It was during this time that they had a common enemy and stood united against the production company, shouting and swearing in unison at the CEO of the production company in times of crisis. Their reconciliation was urgent and necessary. Karim was the mediator between the two often.

The new cooperation between the two divas improved the working environment but never stopped their eternal rivalry and their clashes continued over old feuds or even nothing.

Life went on and Sandrine's name was going from success to success. She had become reconciled to the fact that she was not a spring chicken anymore, and accepted the mature women's role and as she portrayed a mother this made her miss real-life motherhood that she had sacrificed for the sake of fame. She had an intimate moment with her old flame Roger out of the shooting schedule. Suppressed emotions that had been dormant surfaced.

'I wanted to have a child with you, Sandrine,' he said.

'You are digging up old things that are gone.'

'I was very keen to have a long-term relationship with you.'

'But you could not. I caught you flirting with the make-up girls.'

'People forgive.'

'I do not.'

Her statement did not surprise Roger. Sandrine was known for holding grudges. Forgiveness was not listed in her dictionary. It was a moment of contemplation when she asked herself what if I'd had children. Would I have been a good mother? Alas.

She woke up to a gentle tap on her shoulder. She felt the rough masculine hand of Karim caressing her. He was her only solace and comfort. She looked at his sad face that had probably aged before its time and she felt guilty for her self-centered attitude and not thinking about the man who had turned her life upside down for the best. She had felt the taste of happiness after long sombre years of isolation and self-depreciation. But she was aware of not letting her wild dream go on. She was thirty years his senior and he was a devout husband and father.

'You know, I wish we had met before,' she whispered. She touched his blemished olive skin. 'I know your heart is torn between Syria and England.'

'I think you understand. I do not feel I belong here,' he said in a deep faint voice. She turned her back to him and started weeping. He tried to touch her gently but received an angry response. She pushed his hand away fiercely. 'Get out of here,' she shouted. Her wailing attracted unnecessary attention. To Karim's horror, he was scared of the consequences of her reaction and left in haste. Sandrine felt the void without him and shouted at the crew who flocked to her rescue. 'Get out of my sight. I want a drink,' she yelled.

Chapter thirty-eight

A Painful Journey

Summer is exceptionally hot in Southern Turkey. The refugees had been uprooted from their native cities and villages in Syria but mainly from Aleppo and Idlib. The agony those refugees endured was inconceivable.

Fadwa and her young family moved from one camp to another and ended up at Hatay in Turkey near the Syrian border. She had declined any offer from her husband or her immediate family to flee to Europe with the Syrian diaspora when the Turkish authorities opened its borders with Europe despite the desperate attempts of Karim to convince her to the contrary. He conversed with Fadwa when they had the chance to have access to a satellite phone on rare occasions.

'I am not going to leave illegally. We tried it with disastrous consequences. It did not work,' she said in a very emotionally charged voice interrupted with the noise of her rapid breathing.

'Please be reasonable,' he said.

'You are the one who should be. You are parading happily in Paris with a senile women.' Her sarcastic language revealed her jealousy.

'What do you mean?' he replied in fear that she had found out about his affair with Sandrine.

'My brother called me and a friend of his who lives in France mentioned your liaison.'

Karim found it hard to swallow and wished for a sip of water to clear his throat. 'Darling, do not believe rumours. People are jealous because I have a job. She is my employer. Cheer up, I lost the other job. People are envious and it is bad karma. Darling, I am saving every penny for you and the children so we can reunite.' His words mesmerised her, she believed his actions could ruin their marriage. Before Fadwa could reply or recite verses of the Quran to counteract and protect him from the evil spell, the conversation disconnected and it was inconclusive as was always the case. Both were in fear of losing each other. They felt insecure being apart.

But the situation back home was getting dire. The bombing was killing civilians and the casualties were beyond belief. The siege of Aleppo was a historic event with injustice and maximum suffering for the civilians. The non-countable casualties of war terrified Karim who was mesmerised by French TV5, The Al-Jazeera and the British BBC TV channels contradicted the news from the Syrian TV which talked about triumphs, victories and glories of the Syrian Government's army and its success in defeating the enemy. The picture was too complex to comprehend by human beings. The National Front of Liberation of Syria evolved and emerged into another Islamic State. Then Turks, Russians, Iranians and the Gulf Estates backed by the United States and the West had their fingerprints imprinted on these atrocities. 'Enough,' Karim shouted as he threw the remote control violently to ground.

'Are you okay, Karim?' asked his roommate. Karim stood up from the ageing rug where he was sitting on the floor.

'I am not. Are you? Are we all? The whole area is hell. Do you know what has happened to your family? Your parents? I have lost my family.'

His roommate approached Karim and offered him a hug as he tried to comfort him. 'Take it easy. We are all in the same boat. It won't last for long. God will save us.' Karim tried to release himself from his mate's tight but gentle grip.

'How could God let this Hell keep going. It is not fair. God should protect us not cause harm and destruction,' Karim replied.

'Please do not curse God, you and your family will be cursed and shuffled to Hell.' His friend's tone was charged with emotion for fear of the consequences.

'And what do you call this? Isn't it Hell?' Karim muttered the sentence in a sarcastic tone.

The other guy withdrew himself muttering words of forgiveness from God and asking mercy for Karim.

Karim put on his heavy second-hand coat. He'd left all his designer clothes purchased by Sandrine at her flat in a defiant act after their argument. He left the room and started walking in the streets of Belleville, refreshing his face in the chilly early spring wind as he walked aimlessly in the street that looked nicer in the darkness of the evening. He heard murmurs and guessed it was Arabic mixed with Middle-Eastern music. He recognise Shadia, the late Egyptian singer's voice as he came closer to scruffy café frequented by North African migrants. He sniffed the smell of apple-flavoured tobacco smoke, emitted from the shishas mixed with mint tea. He became more alert as if he had woken up from a deep sleep. He dashed into the Moroccan café, hoping to have mint tea the same as his grandmother used to prepare when he was not feeling well as a child. The nostalgic atmosphere of the café drew him inside the crowded place where men were smoking the shisha. It reminded him of his grandfather who used to caress his hair when he used to accompany him to the café in old citadel of Aleppo. He sat comfortably on a wiggly aluminium chair. The young Moroccan waiter, in his early twenties, looked exhausted from a long day of work in return for poor pay. He was wearing jeans and tea-stained apron. He arrived in haste to take Karim's order.

Karim responded to the waiter's greeting with a nod. He ordered green tea. The young man placed the cup of tea on the table and scrutinised the life-battered face of Karim. 'Where are you from, brother?'

'Syria,' Karim responded in a sad tone that the young man hardly could hear.

'Oh, my heart goes out to you and your people.' His genuine tone refreshed Karim.

'Me too.'

'What are you doing in Paris?' The young waiter asked.

'I am a refugee.' Karim made the statement to confirm his legal status.

'I have many Syrian friends. I helped a few to move to England.'

The effect of England was music to his ears despite having numerous encounters with smugglers. The young man smelt Karim's appetite for such a service. 'It is safe, secure and reasonable pricewise.' They exchanged phone numbers.

Karim was reliving his old dream of reaching the promised land but woke to the noise and the screams of the girl who was drowning in the English Channel during his last escape attempt. He woke to the beeping of a text message. He searched for his mobile in the bottom of his pocket and clicked it to display a message.

'Pardon moi,' it said.

He searched the source of the message. It was Sandrine. She must have sought help from others to operate her smartphone. *Do people really change?*

He glanced at her message to ask for forgiveness. He read it again and again in disbelief.

Chapter thirty-nine

La vie en Rose

Karim moved back to Sandrine's flat in Châtelet. Her attempts to re-kindle their relationship were exceptionally successful. She bombarded him with messages and phone calls, having been able to master her smartphone after many desperate attempts. Since she had snapped at him without reason, her aggressive attitude culminated in confrontations with others at work too. Claudette was the number one target with or without provocation. Nevertheless, she learnt to change her tack to smooth the way by apologising at times, using seduction to satisfy Karim's unlimited sexual appetite or asking pity for a helpless old woman. But she never denounced her disgusting and humiliating way of treating others.

'She is the master of manipulation,' Claudette gossiped with her make-up artist.

Equally, Sandrine was keen to live her life in tranquility, away from the studios even though she longed to be there. In an interview with *Paris Match*, she declared that she wanted to have a break and might consider another project in the future. Her fear of loneliness made her consider the studio her home and the crew her family.

'Do you really mean it?' Karim asked with apparent concern.

'Well, you have to be precious for the public to love and miss you. I feel that I am too accessible.' She turned the pages of the glossy magazine. 'I miss the quiet life I have adapted to,' as she eyed old photos of her 1960s films, ruminating about her long-gone gorgeous body and her twenties looks. *I cannot live without the lights.*

She had learnt that she was incapable of coping without Karim. She begged him time and time again to come back and he did eventually, on the condition that he received mutual respect and benefits. Karim needed the money to support his family in Syria in exchange for Sandrine's company. Nonetheless, he missed her rudeness, despite her shouting he realised she had a heart of gold too.

The days went by, eating, drinking, walking and they were a man and a woman trying to live under one roof with their background differences. They had been to restaurants, Southern France, attended invitations to parties and galleries. Overall, Karim gained some acceptance by French society all thanks to Sandrine, even if her approval was conditional on her mood and mental state. He was not innocent and pushed the wrong buttons occasionally. They realised that both of them thrived on action.

Her career renaissance on the French art map gave her a new lease on life. She had interviews on TV and media and even became the *darling* of social media with Karim's help and guidance. The direct cat fights with Claudette transferred to the novel social media tools such Twitter, Facebook and Instagram. Her impulsive, rude and instant responses did not sit well with the politically correct world or the producers but was major entertainment for social media and the public too.

She felt the need to have a man in charge of her though she could not switch her principles that she had learnt from her old acquaintance with the French women's writer and philosopher Simone de Beauvoir about the emancipation of women. Beauvoir had worked relentlessly to promote gender equality all her life.

Needless to say, her association with Karim opened her eyes to others problems and suffering which drove her to work for charities in France and abroad. His plight drew her attention to helping others including the misfortunate refugees fleeing the war. Her recent revived celebrity status made her a patron of charities and organisations. This optimised her satisfaction and reduced her self-centered attitude. Karim was a soft wind blowing in her life, but she knew he was not for her. The mismatch was obvious — culture, background, age — everything. But he was kind and had a calming effect on her. 'I think I love him,' she said to Roger once.

When they arrived late at a charity gala, it didn't matter because Sandrine had become its patron. The charity cared for homeless refugees in Paris. It had been Karim's suggestion and she was grateful to him for her achievement of securing shelters for destitute, forgotten people. It was followed by a business dinner at Maxims for a new production company. The company were planning a new TV series.

'I was bored to death by that old fat producer,' she said as she flopped her tiny body on the sofa next to her dog who ignored her cries.

'Business connections are vital,' Karim said.

But I enjoy the charity work more. They are real people. And it's made me feel good.' She sighed with elation.

'Karim, where are you?' She turned around looking for him like a child seeking her mother.

She heard nothing. She walked barefoot to his room, thinking that he could be using the bathroom. There was no sign of him. The panic was apparent on her face. And despite her debilitating anxieties, she managed to curb them recently since she had revived her long gone *vedette* image. Her panicked voice varied from trembling to high-pitched. 'Karim!

Karim! Where are you?' The silence killed her. She had lost him like all the others. 'It is my fault; I have lost him.' She collapsed on the sofa.

Not long after she heard a strong masculine voice. 'What is the matter? I am here.' Karim's voice came from a distance.

Sandrine rushed to the kitchen and found Karim sitting on the floor and weeping. He was trying to hide the noise generated by his weeping. She bent down with an effort on her weak knees as she tried desperately to reach him.

'What is the matter, darling?' She hugged him tenderly.

'Nothing,' he replied with difficulty.

'Don't try to fool me. Has someone upset you tonight?' Her assertive tone reassured him like a mother attending her baby.

'No, I am upset to hear that the Syrian camps have been bombed.' He wept loudly.

Sandrine felt sorrow as well as a pinch of jealousy about her rival Fadwa. She was resigned to the fact that he would reunite with his family somehow, in some time to come. She knew that his heart was with his wife and children.

'I am sorry, dear. You should not upset yourself. Things will get worse before getting any better.' She uttered her words like a wise woman.

'It is going from bad to worse Sandrine. My hands are tied. I am doing nothing to rescue my family.' He held her hand with a tight grip.

She moved her tiny body closer to his muscular body, and provided him with warmth and a tender touch.

'I did not want to tell you that I have been in touch with the UNHCR, the world refugee agency. My correspondence had been ongoing; I've been trying to find a way to help your family.'

Karim was surprised by her unexpected statement. 'You did all that?' he said as he interrupted her speech. His face showed astonishment and disbelief.

Sandrine looked down at the marble floor and responded with a sigh. 'People think I am very self-centered without a heart. The rigid strong facade you see hides a weak, broken person. Having been appreciated for my looks since early childhood to my days of stardom made me seem a cold, indifferent and rude person. I am just the victim of a ruthless industry and superficial society.'

Karim realised the impact of his revelation on Sandrine. 'I did not mean to …' he said in a quiet calm voice full of shame.

She stopped him with a gesture of her hand; raising to ask him not to continue. 'It is the truth and that is what I like about you. No one has told me that before. I believe I have changed and my life has probably taken a better turn. Who knows.'

Karim approached and hugged her; her mascara tears stained his cheeks. They exchanged kisses as she pulled her tiny body from his strong grip softly. 'We should never give up. That is what you told me. Do you remember my speech at the charity event for the jungle camp refugees?' she whispered.

'What did you say? Well … my French is not up to standard.' His voice amused her when he spoke in broken French.

'That is not true, your French has improved immensely. I think it is better than my English.'

She sat on an old wooden creaking chair. Karim brought her a glass of Bordeaux in a crystal glass. She declined it and asked him to make coffee for two. While he was busy operating the coffee machine by placing the capsule in the machine, she sat like a queen ordering one of her subjects around. The coffee smell calmed them both down. Sandrine took her first sip and lifted her eyebrows in admiration of the coffee and its maker. Karim made a noise while sipping. He stopped as soon as he saw the disapproval on her face. 'Now, let's talk business,' she said.

'What do you mean?'

'I want to leave the emotions aside for a while and be frank. Karim you are not happy here.'

'Well, I'm not sure,' he said and glanced at the floor, as if he was in front of a strict headmistress being shamed for not telling the truth.

'I know where your heart is. It is in England and with your family. My inquiries have revealed that the best way for you to reunite with your family is for you to claim asylum in the UK. It is easier to do than if you try it in France. I agree with you. You would find it easier to assimilate with the society there rather than in France.'

'And you?'

'What about me! I am fine. I have lived my life well and I was lucky to meet you, you have made me appreciate what I have.'

He hugged her, but Sandrine pushed him away gently. 'I realise that you have to reach the UK in an illegal way.'

'You disapprove of what I have done, trying to reach England by using a smuggler.' His voice was full of surprise at Sandrine's U-turn.

'It is very hard for me to say, I was wrong and you were right. But who needs a smuggler,' she said in a tone without pride.

'What do you mean?' he asked in surprise.

'Smugglers are crooks and we can do better.' Her confident tone bewildered him.

'But that needs a lot of arrangement.'

'I am on to it and I have a plan.'

Karim opened his mouth wide.

'Yes and I am going to accompany you.'

'What? You know it is an illegal act and if we are caught the consequences could be dire.' His speech was almost too rapid to catch.

She sipped her coffee. 'Of course I do, calm down.' She took another sip and raised her eyebrows. Karim stared at her in amazement.

Chapter forty

New Start

Paris warmed up with high summer temperatures for the arrival of tourists from all over the world. Parisians were pushed to the provinces in a forced temporary immigration as they fled their elegant city to the comfort of the countryside or the seaside.

The Paris Metro, buses and overground public transport were filled with tourists speaking various languages. This added to the confusion of the endogenous Parisians who prided themselves in speaking only French. Karim's recurrent journeys to Belleville and other parts of Paris did not bother the self-absorbed Sandrine anymore.

He had taught her to use social media, Viber and What's App apps to communicate with him and her fans alike. She found her way into Facebook, Twitter and Instagram with some struggling to start with. Later, she became hooked on the novelty of those toys. He knew that she would get fed up with her new toy as children do.

The conversations about an escape plan were conducted in French, English and even Arabic at times. Sandrine enjoyed the mystery, adventure and the sudden excitement that had come into her life, thanks to Karim. On the other hand, deep down she was mourning the imminent loss of love and companionship

They didn't love one another but rather complemented each other. She thought of her nights of loneliness, self-loathing and isolation. Her only solace was regurgitating the happy memories of her heydays and watching one of her old films. But now her life was full with acting, limelight, charity work and endless invitations.

Planning for an adventure to smuggle Karim was one of her film's adventures that would be acted in real life.

Brighter thoughts crept to her mind when she was in a pleasant mood and lifted her to the moon. Her nomination by the French State for the highest accolade of the La République Française was the height of her life events and a dream come true. While she was in a pensive mode, she heard the key turn and the door open. Sandrine's anxiety mounted. 'Who is it?' she shouted in panic.

'It is me, dear, Karim.' His soft masculine voice was reassuring.

'Oh, you gave me the fright of my life'. She extended her hands calling him to hold her.

He approached and touched her tenderly while she grabbed him and held him tightly to her chest. 'I will miss you,' she said with a sniff.

'You can come and visit me in London,' he said as he gazed at the golden rays shining through the window.

Londres, ma belle ville. I like the city and the shopping is heaven'. She asked Karim in a princely manner to pass her glass of wine. She took a sip to Karim's discontent. He was afraid she would abuse alcohol again. 'You will get to England and hopefully reunite with your family and you will forget this old woman.' She took another sip while he glanced at her image in the venetian mirror on the wall opposite.

He knelt down beside the chaise longue where Sandrine was lying in her nighty and resembled Cleopatra. 'I will never forget your favour as long as I live. You installed hope inside me. I was mortified to venture beyond the painful, failed and traumatic experiences. You made me overcome the fear.'

'You cannot imagine how my confidence was hitting rock bottom when I met you. I am more confident, less anxious and have managed to go back to public life with success.' She uttered her words with confidence that Karim had never noticed before.

'And you stand up to your rivals.' His cheeky tone diluted the seriousness of the subject.

'Like that bitch Claudette, you mean.' They laughed from the heart.

'I will miss you'. Her voice was quiet and depicted painful emotions. She cleared her throat and changed her tone. 'Now to action. Where are we with the plan?' Her militant tone woke them from their dreams. Karim had to go to the promised land and Sandrine had to embark on the adventure of her life. The two went into deep discussions with raised voices, extreme gestures, laughing, tears and hugs. They looked like a very happy couple.

Chapter forty-one

Action Time

Karim continued to hide his anxiety and concern about the escape plan from Sandrine. He was showered with proposals from smugglers, professionals and amateurs, and even imposters, as was always the case. Those who thought of him as the chicken who laid golden eggs, chased him relentlessly with the aim of benefitting from his desperation and his elite contacts. The word spread between refugees and locals about his intention to leave. Prices were hitting the roof. In a moment of sheer desperation, he disclosed his thoughts to Sandrine and how he wished to avoid the failure of their plan.

'Stop your stupid anxiety and man-up. You are exposing yourself and me to the public eye. It means we are fraudsters. It may not have a huge impact on you but it will on me,' Sandrine said as she sipped her drink in haste and showed her anger and disagreement at his banal thinking.

He knelt down and burst into tears. 'I don't know what to do. I am living in a puzzle. I want to stay here, but I want to follow my dream and live in the UK. I need to look after my family and it is the only way if they join me in the UK.'

'Darling. You have to follow your dream and you will achieve it.' Her tender voice was full of sorrow.

'You know my story, my failures. I have tried and I am terrified to do it again. No, not another failure.' He turned his face avoiding her eyes.

She stood up and came closer to him; she caressed his hair. 'Once upon the time there was a young teenage girl who lived in a village in the provinces. As with all her generation, she would work either in the fields or maybe in a shop if she was lucky enough. She was very beautiful but very ambitious. She has exchanged kisses with the mayor's son in exchange for watching TV when there were very few households that had TV in the early 1950s. She watched the stars and wanted to be the second Marlene Dietrich and reach Hollywood and conquer its throne. Sometimes she was lucky enough to accompany her mother for Christmas shopping to the town nearby and see her French and Hollywood heroines on the big screen or at the TV shop and rarely at the local small cinema. France had just came out of a horrendous war and everything was scarce.' She had another sip of her drink and glanced at the window, then continued.

'I remember when I was first picked for a small role, the producer laughed and asked how could a scruffy peasant like me play such a role. The same person begged me with an open cheque to play a role in his production a few years later. *'C'est la vie.'* She picked up a Gitanes filter cigarette and gestured for Karim to lighten it for her. He did. It was her way of alleviating her anxiety.

She took another sip of her drink. 'I know you went through a lot in your native country and here. It is not the end. It is the beginning. Look at me. After all I have achieved, I am back to fighting and that's thanks to you. It is my turn to return the favour.'

'What can you do?'

'I am an old fragile, weak and helpless woman. This is what you and many others think about me. No, I am not and I will prove you all wrong.' She raised her crystal glass in a triumphant gesture of celebration, accepting the challenge.

'What are you up to?'

'While you have been wasting your time with bogus smugglers whose main aim is to use vulnerable people like you, I have a plan and you need to listen and learn well. Now, your French is better, if anything very good, and that is the first hurdle we have overcome. It is an additional bonus to be Sandrine's partner. I have asked an old friend who is a cameraman of Algerian descent to prepare travel documents for you. And I have had to apply for a passport, mine expired a long time ago. I have not left France for many years.' Her tone was mixed with excitement and sadness.

'What's in your mind?' Karim could not hide his confusion.

She stood upright and in a very theatrical gesture made an announcement. 'You will see what Sandrine is capable of. I am not weak and feeble anymore.' She extended her hand, showing well-manicured nails and held his cold hand and gave him a kiss on his cheek.

'I will miss you, but I know you cannot be happy here.' Her voice was deep and sad.

'But, I can stay with you, if you …'

'No, Sandrine is proud and independent and will continue to be so. I would rather remember you happily in my memory rather than being miserable with me,' she interrupted him abruptly.

He kissed her mouth and touched tongue with immense passion. She reciprocated the passion by sucking his lips.

In the midst of her ecstasy, she could not bypass the occasion without comment. 'By the way your bouche-à-bouche kiss has improved since you learnt it my way. I am the expert, you know'. She raised her glass.

The good old diva is back.

Chapter forty-two

The Escape Plan

Sandrine had never been so busy or so happy. She felt as if she had a purpose in life, not only helping Karim but having a goal and hopes. She had the taste for excitement and adventure but above all, the satisfaction she gained from giving help made her forget her obsession with herself, her selfishness and to a degree losing Karim was a minor matter.

He revealed his plans after his discussions with smugglers whose charges were astronomical but would they deliver? She told Karim off when he came up with several plans. Once the conversation become so heated on an exceptionally hot early summer's day that the neighbours heard inappropriate shouts of rage from Sandrine.

'You fool, they will kill you and take your money. They do not care what happens to you.' She was about to slap him.

'You do not want me to leave,' he replied as tears filled his eyes.

'Silly boy, you are really stupid. I could have informed the police or the immigration if I wanted that and see who they will listen to.' Her tone was threatening. His mind wandered in different directions. *Is she the right person to trust? It is too late.*

Sandrine's sharp mind picked up his doubts and concerns. She pushed her tiny body over the sofa to come closer to him. 'Darling, trust me. I want to help. I think that I have matured enough in the last few months and it is equivalent to my seventy-seven years of life. I reiterate for the hundredth time that I want you to be with me, but I know you would not be happy and that I cannot stand living with others misery anymore. You need to listen to my opinion and advice.' She touched his thick, unkempt moustache gently. She asked him to hand her the laptop from the adjacent table.

To his surprise she switched it on and logged in to a search machine.

'I have been investigating routes and reading evidence of those who have tried to cross the Channel, both winners and losers. I mean the successful and failed ones. So, I am compiling information and evidence about routes of escape from multiple sources and gathering statements from those who succeeded and those who failed to cross, as you can see.' She showed him a saved file loaded with reports in French and English. She asked him to pass her reading glasses. He handed her the malaky designer reading glasses with signs of astonishment on his face at her unexpected efficiency. She pointed at the report with maps to cross the sea where it was dangerous. 'Inflated boats stand only a small chance of success. The British Government is guarding their coast vigorously despite the probably deliberately relaxed French grip on the matter and that is what we are going to use.'

'I have spoken to a guy who will take me to a smuggler,' Karim said as he waited in fear of her furious reaction.

'Here we go again. Who are they; will they give guarantees? I thought we were done with them.'

'He said he would.'

'How much?'

'Three thousand US dollars.'

'Mon Dieu, It is a lot of money for you especially.'

'It is indeed.'

'Well, it is not too much if he secures your trip to England.' She wanted to comfort him with false hope. 'Possibly.' She tried lift her tiny body from the sofa with difficulty. 'I will foot the bill but on one condition. I want to meet the smuggler.'

'Sandrine, do you know the risk this entails? Your reputation and the scandal.' He was shuddering and shaking.

Je m'en fou. If anything, scandals have boosted my career.' She smirked ready for the challenge.

Chapter forty-three

Meeting in Bois De Boulogne

The summer continued to be generous to Paris with the sun spreading its golden rays until the beginning of autumn with longer daylight that perked up the Parisian mood. The Parisians had enjoyed an exceptional summer and some had deferred their plans to flee to the South of France temporarily. The dog walkers embarked on a task of walking their pets early in the morning; they were preceded by the rush of the last hours of work of the Latino transgender prostitutes whose clients tended to be married men, seeking exotic excitement in the mobile vans owned by the prostitutes.

After dark, the place was riskier to venture in. At times it was infested with drug dealers and armed men.

Just before sunset, a taxi stopped close to edge of the Bois de Boulogne next to the main road. The faint dusk light made vison difficult between the trees that varied from oaks to cedar to cherry.

Karim exited the car after paying the driver. He opened the other passenger door and a black Christian Louboutin stiletto touched the muddy ground much to Sandrine's discomfort. Karim held her hand gently, assisting her to gain her balance. Anxiety showed on his face while she was calm and composed.

'Where is he?' Sandrine's voice echoed in the forest like the witch waiting for Hansel and Gretel.

Karim opened his mobile and tried to dial and text the smuggler without success. He had asked the mobster to meet his girlfriend but gossip travels fast among the immigrant society. The desperate refugees knew about Karim's relationship with the famous vedette Sandrine La Croix. All the roads were paved with gold.

When the mystery man did not show up Karim received a bollocking from Sandrine. 'I told you. He is a fraud. You are a fool. He is the lowest of the low.'

'Maybe he is afraid it is a trap and he is afraid of you.'

'Me? I am poor woman who is trying to help.' Her voice was a mixture of disappointment, anger and righteousness. She wanted to prove to Karim how stupid he was. Her raised voice attracted the attention of passersby while her gestures and dress code attracted the working girls who approached with curiosity. A middle-aged white working girl wearing heavy make-up recognised her. 'You are Sandrine the 1960s and 1970s icon. The good times.' The other girls rushed forward wanting to kiss her. Sandrine was scared. Where they clean? She posed for selfies with the girls, but that was all. 'You know, madame, you are an icon for the gays and LGBT's not only in France but in the English and Spanish speaking countries too,' said one girl in a high-pitched Spanish accent.

She was soon surrounded by a crowd. She added excitement to their monotonous, boring high-risk way of living.

Sandrine praised their sense of fashion and turned to Karim. 'Would you sleep with these girls if you had the chance?'

'Yes certainly; they are sexy. But never as sexy as you.' He said these words to please her and hide his sorrow. He was disappointed that he had lost his one and maybe only opportunity of fleeing France to the UK. No money in the world would help him hire illegal smugglers' services. He had been black listed by them and all the immigrant community now.

Chapter forty-four

Planning is Ongoing

The next day Sandrine woke to the smell of espresso filling the air from the newly installed coffee machine that Karim was operating. She was singing Édith Piaf's favourite song' *Tu me fais tourner la tête*'. Her moves were well choreographed and resembled her 1960s hit musical. She was trying to master her moves with great attention while not breaking her hip. She remembered when she met Piaf at a party in Paris. She had aged before her time from abusing alcohol and other illicit substances. Back then Sandrine had been very young, almost a teenager and trying to find her way in the arts' world. She had been accompanied by a producer who promised her stardom in exchange of sexual favours.

She woke from her ruminations to Karim's manly voice, *'Bonjour.'* He presented the coffee to her with a small smile full of disappointment. He offered her a fresh croissant that he had purchased from the local boulangerie. She pushed it away with a look of discontent. He passed the newspapers to her. 'Would you like to read them?'

She glanced at her photos on the wall reflecting on the fifty years of her career. They told a story of success, sadness and loneliness. 'I am too old,' she whispered trying to hide her comment from Karim.

Her blue eyes scanned the newspaper headlines in *Paris Match*. *Sandrine de La Croix is comforting the LGBT community in Paris.* Her eyes rapidly followed the other smaller headlines. *Sandrine is showing her caring side.* Deep down she realised that publicity was rewarding.

Karim pressed a button on his mobile and showed her the Facebook and Twitter posts with photos of her in the Bois du Boulogne. Her image could match Mother Teresa.

Moments later, various phones started ringing and breaking the silence, and bringing Sandrine back to earth. All of a sudden, her agent's attention had grown hugely. He was letting her know that she had a good selling point and producers were jumping in all directions to get her in their productions before the bubble of attention burst.

She was smiling happily and ignoring Karim's bitter expression. She had it all now. She was in a win-win situation, benefiting from the poor transexual prostitutes. In her hype of happiness she turned to him. 'Darling. Don't despair. It is a golden opportunity to get you out of this country.'

'How?'

'I have a plan'

'Smugglers refuse to take me. They think I am a government grass, having come to the attention of the public eye. Thanks to you.' He turned his despairing face to the wall.

'You will thank me soon,' she cooed in a frosty tone as she moved her leg towards his crotch and smirked. 'Please pass me the croissant.' She ate half of the croissant happily without thinking about the calories.

Karim opened his mouth wide. 'Where has all this confidence come from?'

Chapter forty-five

Gare Du Nord (All Aboard)

The Peugeot taxi sped towards the Gare du Nord, the busiest train station in France, weaving its way between the heavy traffic in Paris. The station has been serving passengers to France since the 1840s, as well as other European countries including the UK since the last century.

Crowds and crowds of passengers were arriving at the station, boarding the trains while others were disembarking. The cafés and restaurants were filled with passengers and those who were meeting and greeting or saying goodbye.

The taxi stopped by the main door of the station. The chauffeur got out and rushed to open the door in competition with Karim who was very distraught and preoccupied about his coming trip as he dwelt on its details and ramifications. A high-heeled diva with fine slender legs, snatched from a twenty-something girl emerged from the door. Sandrine showed off her fine, slim figure with a Versace white dress and a matching Venetian lace hat. She walked into the station like a long-gone diva who was coming back to life. It was as though she said. *Look, I am here, alive and kicking.* Karim was carrying two small suitcases while the porter followed with the rest of the Louis Vuitton cases, only fit for a diva. She smiled at the curious onlookers, thinking they were her fans. She might have been well recognised by the older generation, but her recent TV series and her fights with Claudette combined with the recent media attention brought the younger generation's attention too.

Karim was shaking and sweating. His failed attempts to reach the UK played like a horror film in his mind. He was about to call it a day and go back to live with Sandrine or even in his shared room in Belleville.

Sandrine sensed his high level of anxiety, having suffered panic attacks and other mental health problems. She held his sweaty hand tightly. 'Cheri, we live once only. Never give up on your dream.' Her tone was determined.

I have failed twice,' he whispered as he held her hand tighter.

'You will get what you want if you try. People do regret not trying, but not failing.'

'Please carry the suitcases to the train,' she called to the porter.

Sandrine opened her Dolce and Gabbana handbag and checked the passports. She placed her French passport with the maroon colour cover over his blue United Nations refugee travel document, as if she was trying to hide a shameful document from the customs officer's sight. She approached the custom's desk holding Karim's hand tightly. She squeezed his sweaty hand and tapped it with her thumb and forefinger.

She examined the customs officers. A young white man with a blond hair and beside him, an olive-skinned, middle-aged woman who could be of Maghreb origin and then a younger white girl. She darted towards the woman of North African origin.

'*Bonjour*. Gare du Nord is extremely busy today.' She fanned her blonde hair with her Chinese silk, hand fan to make an impression.

'It is always like this, but you know it is the Easter holidays and the Parisians flock to snatch London sales' bargains.' The controller smiled and glanced at Sandrine with curiosity.

'Your face is familiar, mam.' The middle-aged inspector uttered her words with hesitation.

'Ha! Ha! *Bien sûr,* do you watch cinema and TV?' She straightened her posture, showing her slim and fine figure to the woman as if she was a model in the fashion show. This attracted the attention of other passengers whereas her mission had been to distract the customs official, but she could not deny she was enjoying the glare of fame.

'Sandrine, is that you? You look wonderful.' The old clerk of the train company was taken by surprise by one of the icons of French cinema.

'*Oui,* it is me. You got it right.' Sandrine's reply was a proud one.

'Here you are, madame.' She handed her the two passports without opening them.

'*Merci.*' Sandrine had achieved the first step of her plan and escorted Karim to the departure gates. She put the passports inside her handbag.

'By the way, my mother adored you. She used to watch you in her native country Morocco before emigrating to France. The custom's officer announced loudly, showing some Dutch courage.

Sandrine did not appreciate the last comment and gave the woman with an unappreciative look.

She turned in panic and looked for Karim. '*Merde!*' she swore, dashing away aimlessly as she looked for her lover as if looking for her toddler. To her surprise she spotted Karim talking to a policeman. She sped up her pace as she struggled to walk in her stilettos.

'Karim, *cheri,* where are you? Her raised voice attracted the porter who was pushing the trolley towards first class. Karim rushed to her and grasped her arms. She tried to reach his mouth which seemed a distance away for her shorter stature. She wanted to kiss him.

'Darling the customs officer stopped me and asked for my travel documents,' he said fearfully.

'*Bonjour*, madame. Is the gentleman with you?' The middle-aged man wearing an old grey suit showed his ID and identified himself as an immigration officer.

'*Bien sûr*. He is my husband,' she replied in a bossy raised tone as she lifted her eyebrows in made-up astonishment.

'Madame, may I dare to ask you a question?' he asked with fear of reprisal.

'Fire away,' she replied in an abrupt tone.

'Forgive my curiosity. Are you Sandrine?' the officer asked with hesitation.

'*Oui.*' Her tone perked up.

'Can I ask you for an autograph?'

He handed a dated diary with a pen. She touched it with discontent for fear of contamination from germs but signed her autograph confidently.

'My father adores you. It will make his day. He is living a boring life in a nursing home and nothing will cheer him up like your autograph,' he said to her before departing triumphantly.

Sandrine pulled a face. She turned around looking for Karim among the passengers hurrying before the train departed.

'Where have you been? I thought I had lost you.' She tried to hide her anger.

'I'm sorry. I was fearful that he would detain me.' He followed her like a baby lamb in a herd of sheep.

Listen, do not leave my sight.' Her tone showed power and control.

They walked hand in hand until Karim took over the trolley from the porter who had to stay behind the security barrier. Karim continued pushing it and dragged different size bags to the first class compartment of the Eurostar where the train conductor was waiting to greet them warmly as if he was ready to roll out the red carpet.

'*Bonjour,* madame,' he said with a friendly smile as he extended his hand to Sandrine and helped her to get into the coach, before he escorted her to her seat.

'Karim, the tickets.' Karim produced the prime Eurostar tickets out of his blue jacket and handed them to the conductor who welcomed the couple in French with a broad smile, showing his nicotine-stained teeth in contrast to the colour of his blond moustache. They settled in the train as guard's whistle announced the departure of the train. Karim was trembling like a leaf in the wind.

'Darling it's over,' she said in a sexy whisper.

The train hostess arrived with a smile. 'Drinks madame?'

'Just the time.' Sandrine's hands were shaking with a mixture of anxiety and alcohol need.

'What would you like?' the young French woman was used to surprises from clients like.

'Chardonnay for two please.'

The girl rushed to fulfil her order.

'Voila, madame,' the pretty hostess presented the drinks on a tray with a chicken casserole and boiled potatoes and cheese and crackers. Sandrine picked up the wine and the salad. She downed her glass of wine in record time to the hostess' astonishment.

'Another glass please.' The young girl hurried to bring the order.

'Are you okay, Karim? Have a drink.' She turned to him after the alcohol had calmed her nerves.

'I am worried.' He picked at a small piece of bread and brie, He was filled with guilt.

'What is your problem? We have passed through British customs. You are safe.' She called the hostess for more wine.

Karim was quiet. A short time later, the train went into the tunnel under the sea and the microphone announced that they were crossing the English Channel. Sandrine held his hand firmly. 'We are free, darling.'

For Karim the trip took forever. But Sandrine was rejuvenated by the buzz of excitement and fear combined, and enjoyed the adrenalin rush. *It is the end. Sandrine will be alone again.*

The light struck Sandrine's green eyes once the train came out of the tunnel. She looked for her sunglasses in her Prada case. She sipped the wine slowly as she watched the green fields of the English countryside.

'Here you are. Fulfil your dream. We are in England.'

Karim looked around. He stood up and bent over Sandrine as he looked through the window at his promised land. 'It is real. I am in England.' He voiced the happy end of his nightmare so loudly that that it brought anger to Sandrine's face. 'Shut up. You are attracting unnecessary attention.' She looked around, making sure that he had not been heard. Karim ignored her and his excitement continued. She pulled him by his collar and gave him a long kiss sealing his mouth to shut him up. The kiss seemed very hot and drew the other passenger's attention. It was a head-turning scene many could not ignore.

Nevertheless, the kiss served its purpose by calming him down. She stuffed a cheese sandwich into his mouth and he ate it together with sparse sips wine as he ignored his feelings of religious guilt.

'You have to pretend you are a westerner to get rid of unnecessary attention,' she said in a bossy tone like a headteacher, addressing a naughty student.

Karim felt the hours were passing slowly. He gazed at Sandrine who was having a nap after her heavy boozing session. He examined her face, wrinkles softened with Botox but even so she retained her former beauty. While Karim had not passed out under the influence of alcohol, Sandrine was making a light noise with her cat-like snoring. Then the loudspeakers announced the approach to Saint Pancras Station.

Sandrine woke from her light nap to find Karim shaking like a leaf at the sound from the loudspeaker. His face was terrified.

'What's wrong with you? We are in London.' She held his sweaty hand tightly.

'Really? I cannot believe it. I have been looking forward to this all my life and now it is true,' he said overloaded with fear and happiness.

'Life is like a wheel. One day up, the other down. It cannot stay the same,' she whispered.

'I cannot believe my eyes.' He turned to examine his surroundings, looking behind his back in anticipation of being caught by security or border guards.

'Now, stay put. I have not been to London for a long while but I have never encountered problems.' She drank what was left of her white wine.

'Is it a beautiful city?' he asked in excitement mixed with anticipation.

'Lovely city. Very unique. I remember shooting a film at Pinewood Studios. The Brits never got used to having a French vedette in the industry. Actually, I was not very famous in France back then.'

Karim frequented the toilet several times to alleviate his immense anxiety before his bladder.

'Be careful. You are looking suspicious,' Sandrine whispered.

'I am terrified.'

'It should be alright.' Her confident voice reassured him.

The conductor asked Karim if he wanted a drink. 'No thank you,' he replied while Sandrine extended her arms and asked for more white wine.

Not long after, the announcements in English and French said the train would soon stop at St Pancras Station. Karim wanted to rush to the toilet, but Sandrine held his hand firmly and stopped him.

'Listen. I will tell you a story. Actually, it is the story of my life. I remember the first time I went for an audition in Paris. I came from my village in Southern France. I was a mere peasant hardly recognised by the Parisians. They made fun of my clothes, my etiquette and my method of acting. But I stayed put and worked hard. And later, I made fun of all of them.' She raised her glass of wine and toasted for her victory before downing the whole lot in one go, like a thirsty camel in the desert.

The train entered the Victorian St Pancras Station, which was built in 1868. The Andalusian arches reminded him of the Umayyad Mosque in Damascus. The train slowed down and came to a halt. The loudspeakers announced, 'Welcome to Saint Pancras, London.'

'On y va, Karim, let's go. I have booked at the Dorchester.' She increased the volume of her voice to draw some attention and distraction too and to show off her important figure.

Karim's shaking hands could hardly carry Sandrine's Louis Vuitton suitcases, which were heavy.

'I do miss the London shopping. It is heaven,' she said loudly, attracting more attention. She was thinking of her acting mentor Pierre, who taught her to project her voice to reach her audience in the theatre.

Karim off-loaded the suitcases and looked for a porter to help. A group of senior French women started whispering, stealing looks at Sandrine and her toy boy. Then, Karim and Sandrine departed from the coach. Karim held her hand and she felt the tremor transmitted to her hand and body respectfully.

'Hold on. We are here. Well done.' She did not know where her strength came from. Her looks and gesticulations turned the heads of the passengers as any diva would.

While she was walking holding Karim's hand they were followed by the porter. Just then a young, white, tall Englishman with black hair and dark blue eyes, who was showing his muscular arms and his beer belly from his white shirt spoke. 'Hello, welcome to London. Are you just visiting?' he addressed Karim who had stumbled.

Sandrine realised that he must be a customs' officer in disguise. While Karim's tongue was paralysed, the customs officer's suspicion mounted.

'Monsieur, I am Sandrine, the Francophone and Anglo Saxon world star. I am sure you have heard of me. The French and the world cinema icon. *La plus célèbre du monde.* Her words struck poor customs' officer as if he had been punched. He was so taken by surprise that he gave Karim a miss. The raised volume of her voice attracted the curiosity of some French passengers who dared to come closer. An older French woman politely requested her autograph. Another younger girl took a snapshot with her smartphone without her permission. The crowd grew bigger and bigger as did the noise. A young French man introduced himself as a journalist from *Paris Match* and said he wanted to interview her, much to her delight. He immediately started asking her questions about her recent come back and if her arrival to London was a publicity stunt. 'How do you rate yourself as an actress?' he asked.

She answered and glanced at the horizon where Karim was disappearing among the crowd.

'A diva. The diva is always a diva.' She uttered the words with eyes filled with tears.

THE END

Lightning Source UK Ltd.
Milton Keynes UK
UKHW010850070922
408462UK00001B/129